BECKY

A Jack Kendall Mystery

She escaped the cartel—but can
she escape her darkest fears?

JAY B. GREENE

Contents

For Tynan, Casey and Jordan

Boketon Press

ISBN (Paperback): 979-8-9902256-2-6
ISBN (eBook): 979-8-9902256-3-3

Book Design by Adam Hay Studio, UK
E-Pub Formatting by Steve Mead Graphic Design

Printed in the United States of America

Chapter 1:
Morning in Bogotá

9 a.m., Monday, Jan. 5, 1981

Becky Kendall sat in a comfortable chair on the porch of her three-bedroom luxury apartment that overlooked Bogotá's upscale Zona Rosa neighborhood.

As she sipped her steaming cappuccino, street vendors below sold tourists food, jewelry, bags, and traditional handicrafts. She took a slow sip, savoring the warm taste, while her thoughts drifted back to the horrendous firefight in the Blue Mountains—a firefight in which she barely escaped with her life.

The pop of gunfire, the blasts of rockets, and the sickening cry of men dying came back with jarring clarity. Becky tightened her grip on the mug, sweat forming on her forehead as her memories replayed.

"Breathe," she reminded herself. "That's over now. I'm here. I survived."

She looked for calm in the street scene. Zesty and flavorful aromas filled the air as patrons ordered breakfast in nearby cafés and restaurants. She soaked in the calm scene of one of South America's greatest cities, a striking contrast to the traumatic two weeks spent in Jamaica's Blue Mountains.

Mornings like this, sitting on her balcony with the sunlight warming her face, brought her a brief reprieve. Yet, a moment later, her thoughts inevitably returned to the pain she felt.

Nearly six months after escaping the firefight, Becky still couldn't shake the haunting memories of leaving her husband, Jack, and accepting Robert Mackey's invitation to go to Jamaica.

After she arrived in Bogotá, she received good news from her Jamaican friend, Rosa, that Mackey had died during the battle on the mountain between two rival drug gangs.

She felt no sadness, only relief.

When she considered how wrong she had been, she thanked her lucky stars for the opportunity to visit Jamaica with her childhood friend from Chicago, Michelle Talley.

Despite the trauma, Becky found a silver lining in the ordeal; Michelle kept her promise and gave Becky half the $5 million her former fiancé, Michael LeCare, who also died during the battle, had left in their joint bank account in Bogotá.

But the illicit cocaine money was not enough. She needed another change. What, she wasn't sure yet, but she couldn't shake the sense that something inevitable was coming.

Chapter 2:
A Day in the Country

11 a.m., Monday, Jan. 5, 1981

Michelle woke up late, as usual. She entered the kitchen, poured herself a cup of coffee, and joined Becky on the balcony.

"So, there you are," she said. "Your favorite spot in the morning, isn't it?"

"Yes, you know me. It is very relaxing out here," Becky replied.

"What would you like to do today?" Michelle asked.

"You've promised to take me on a day trip to that Salt Cathedral in Zipaquirá. How about that? I've been thinking a lot this morning, and it is getting me depressed again," Becky explained.

"It's about Jack, right?" Michelle asked. "I told you to write that letter to him."

"I'm still thinking about it, but now I want to do something different. Can we?" Becky pleaded.

"Sure, we should go to Zipaquirá," Michelle assured her. "I'll call my travel agent to see if we can book a tour bus trip today."

Michelle walked back inside the living room and picked up the phone.

"Hello, Maria? This is Michelle Talley. When is the next bus to Zipaquirá? I need two tickets for the bus and two for the salt mine. Oh. Well, we just decided to go," she said, listening to Maria. "And the taxi will take us home after the tour? Thanks. We will come down to your office shortly."

"What happened?" said Becky as she entered the living room and overheard the end of the conversation.

"Maria said the last bus left an hour ago. She said we could hire a taxi to take us there and back. We need to dress and go to her office. She'll have a taxi waiting for us in 30 minutes."

Becky smiled. "I will shower quickly and be ready in ten," she said.

*　*　*

Becky and Michelle hurried out of their apartment building. They had planned a full day's excursion to Zipaquirá and had no time to waste.

As they crossed the street, they passed an American man with a thick black mustache wearing a white suit and dark sunglasses. He stood smoking a cigarette and pretended to read a newspaper while eyeing the two tall, well-dressed women.

Once they passed, the man set his newspaper down and began following them.

The walk to Maria's Tours took the women less than ten minutes. The man watched as Michelle paid Maria 300 pesos for a round-trip taxi ride and 50 pesos for two entry tickets to the salt mine. He then hailed a taxi of his own.

"All you have to do is tip the driver. One hundred pesos should be enough, but you can give more or less if you want," Maria said.

Michelle thanked Maria, and she and Becky got into the waiting taxi. The driver was told where to go and that they were in a hurry.

Meanwhile, the man with the mustache gave his own driver a hundred-dollar bill and told him not to lose the taxi with Becky and Michelle.

As Becky and Michelle's taxi navigated the busy downtown streets, the driver began to pick up speed as if he were in the Daytona 500.

"What is your name, señor?" Becky asked.

"Jose."

"You speak English?" she said.

"Sí, many drivers who work for Maria must speak English, as she has many American, Canadian, and British clients. Is there something you want to know?"

"Yes, but you don't have to drive so fast. We are getting a late start, but we want an enjoyable ride," Becky said.

"Lo siento, señorita. I'll slow down. I was told you were in a hurry," Jose murmured, glancing nervously in the rearview mirror.

"We missed the tour bus ride this morning. We want to see Zipaquirá and the Salt Cathedral. All in one afternoon," Becky said, her voice tinged with urgency.

"I see," Jose replied, his hands tightening around the

steering wheel. He was somewhat distracted by the taxi following him, turn for turn, as he drove outside the city.

"What can you tell us about where we are going?" Michelle asked, her excitement mixed with curiosity, oblivious to the potential danger behind them.

Jose set aside his concern about the cab following him for the moment. He didn't want to alarm Becky and Michelle, but needed to be careful. He had been stopped and robbed several times when carrying affluent American passengers.

"I've been there many times with my family. The Salt Cathedral is a beautiful and holy place. It is a Catholic Church built more than 600 feet in the tunnels and chambers of an old salt mine.

"I tell people it is the world's ninth wonder, and many agree. Tourists love the peace they feel as they walk deep within the earth.

"Are either of you Catholic? You don't need to be, but for Colombians who believe in Jesus Christ and his sacrifices on the cross, we make many pilgrimages here on Sundays, especially during the 40 days of Lent."

"We aren't Catholics but were raised as Christians," Michelle said.

"The Salt Cathedral is a holy place for us, but you will also enjoy the splendid architecture and learn about Colombian culture and history," Jose said.

"Do people really break down in tears in the cathedral?" Becky asked.

"Sí. It can be overwhelming because of its significance to our lives and families. You should know some basic things. First, the temple has three sections, representing the birth, life, and death of Jesus. Your tour guide will explain as you walk through," Jose said.

"The first section has the 14 Stations of the Cross and the Rosary Chapel. The second section shows the birth of Jesus, his baptism, and the waterfall symbolizing the Jordan River. The central section features the main church with many pews and the largest cross you will probably ever see. It is an incredible sight."

Becky asked, "Do they allow us to take pictures? I brought my camera."

"Sí. There are many colors because of the lights and the way the salt glistens. You can take pictures. My children love the cool, dark atmosphere and the idea of going inside the earth. To them, it is spooky. To us, we love the salt sculptures and feeling you are closer to Jesus," said Jose as he made the sign of the cross with one hand.

As the three talked and passed the time, Jose drove through the scenic Colombian countryside, past farmlands, rolling hills, lush green forests, and small towns and villages.

Jose watched the taxi in the rearview mirror. It was still keeping a safe distance behind. They could make it without being stopped.

"Is that the Andes?" Becky asked.

"Sí, it is the longest mountain range in the world. Did you know that? In Colombia, some of those peaks rise 19,000 feet above sea level. It isn't Mount Everest at 29,000 feet, but it is very tall," Jose said with a chuckle.

As Becky gazed at the Andes ahead, she recalled last summer's Blue Mountains of Jamaica.

"Would you like me to take you there one day?" he asked.

Becky shuddered at the thought.

"I think I have been in enough mountains for the time

being," she said. "I grew up in Chicago, but I lived for a time in Florida. It's all very different than this country."

"Well, anytime you want to drive through the mountains, I can take you," Jose said.

"Maybe one day," Becky said. "For now, we will see Zipaquirá. It is close enough to the mountains for me."

As he drove under a clear blue sky, the road turned gently through vibrant fields dotted with small farms and grazing livestock. The air felt fresher, and the scenery was more vivid than they could've imagined. As they passed small towns, colorful buildings and charming plazas could be seen.

After about 45 minutes, Jose said they were getting close to Zipaquirá. As they approached, the terrain became more mountainous. On the outskirts of the town, they started to see the classical colonial styles of the houses and whitewashed buildings.

"Here we are. Zipaquirá. Did you want me to drop you off somewhere in particular?" Jose asked.

"Yes," said Michelle. "We want to do some sightseeing first. Where would be a good place?"

"I could drop you near the central square—the Plaza de los Comuneros," Jose said. "This is something for you to see. There are shops and restaurants all around. It is maybe a 20-minute walk to the Salt Cathedral. It will not be hard to find. Everybody knows where it is."

"That sounds good. Take us there," Michelle said. "Becky, are you hungry? Maybe we could get some coffee, freshen up, and get something to eat?"

"Sure, sounds good," Becky said. "It was a nice drive, but I could use some food."

After several minutes, Jose drove through the town, pulled

over, and stopped. He looked into his rearview mirror and saw the taxi following them stop as well.

"That is the plaza. There are restaurants all around," Jose said.

"Thank you, Jose. You've been very helpful. Here is a small tip. Please pick us up at the Salt Cathedral at four o'clock," Becky said.

"Sí, Señorita Becky," said Jose, taking the dollar bill.

Becky and Michelle opened the back door and got out of the cab.

Jose paused for a moment, then got out of the cab, walked around and approached the two women. "Hold on, I must tell you this."

Surprised, Becky's heart skipped a beat. He seemed worried. "Is everything okay?" she asked, trying to sound firm.

Jose frowned. "I don't want to alarm you, but I suspect a taxi followed us from Maria's."

Becky froze. "What did you say?"

"It's probably nothing," Jose said quickly, though his unease was apparent. "A coincidence, perhaps. But...you should be careful."

Michelle stepped closer. "Are they still here?" she asked, wondering what to do.

Jose shook his head, lowering his voice. "No. The taxi left a few minutes ago. But I saw an American man step out—a tall man in a white suit and hat. He walked away down the side street behind you."

Becky exchanged a tense glance with Michelle. "An American?" she repeated. "Why would he be following us?"

Jose shook his head. "I'm not sure. He could be sightseeing, like you two." He looked back to the street, then back to Becky.

"I don't like coincidences. And here, we say it's better to be cautious than sorry."

Becky's stomach churned. "What should we do?"

"For now, stay alert. Don't trust strangers, even if they seem friendly. And if anything feels wrong, find a police officer or go somewhere crowded." Jose hesitated, then added, "I don't want to scare you, but this city has its dangers. You can't always tell friend from foe."

Michelle clutched Becky's arm, her voice shaking. "Becky... what if it's..."

"We don't know anything yet," Becky cut her off, though her pulse thundered in her ears.

Jose stepped back, giving them a reassuring wave, though his expression remained tense. "Take care of yourselves."

As he turned and walked away, Becky and Michelle stood still.

"What do we do now?" Michelle whispered.

Becky swallowed hard, forcing herself to steady her breathing. "We keep moving. And we watch for anyone in a white suit."

Chapter 3:
Gordo's Plan

Gordon "Gordo" Gecht had waited months to confront Becky and Michelle.

But now, sitting in an outdoor café across the street from the penthouse where Becky and Michelle were hiding, he knew patience would be his most valuable weapon. Rushing in could cost him. These women might recognize him from Sarasota, where he'd been the chief enforcer for Robert Mackey's now-defunct cocaine ring based at the High Seas Restaurant on Siesta Key. He couldn't afford any mistakes.

Months of planning had brought him to this point. Months of seething in Miami, watching the news of Mackey's empire crumbling piece by piece. Each headline reminded him of what he'd lost, and each one fueled his resolve.

Revenge would come in time. For now, he needed to focus on the money. The Colombian account held the key to rebuilding his life, but to access it, he needed the women alive—at least for a little while.

But Becky wasn't just a target for Gordo—she was bait. Where Becky went, husband Jack Kendall would be sure to follow. He did so in Jamaica, and he would do so in Bogotá.

Gordo remembered Jack from the old days, the high-powered journalist who always seemed to be in places he shouldn't have been, asking questions no one wanted to answer.

He blamed Kendall and his newspaper, the *Sarasota Herald-Tribune*, for reporting on the High Seas drug ring and Mackey, leading to the busts.

If Jack were to come looking for Becky in Bogotá, it would be the perfect opportunity to deal with him once and for all.

Gordo's ambitions in Bogotá extended beyond Becky, Michelle, and Jack. His ultimate goal was to forge new ties with Pablo Escobar, the man who had supplied Mackey's cocaine paste for years. A partnership with Escobar would ensure Gordo's place at the table in the drug trade, giving him the resources and protection he needed to rise again.

But beneath his calculated plans simmered deep, festering anger. The raid on Mackey's cocaine trafficking operation six months earlier had forced Gordo to flee Sarasota like a cornered rat. He'd lost everything—his network, reputation, and future. The only thing he'd managed to take was $50,000 in emergency cash.

The night of the raid replayed in his mind as he moved through the crowded streets of Bogotá. Hours before federal agents swarmed the High Seas, Gordo had packed a bag, climbed into his car, and driven to Miami.

There, he'd crafted a new identity from scratch. His once-blond hair was dyed black, a thick mustache concealed his face, and a phony passport gave him freedom of movement.

Even so, every headline about the bust felt like a dagger in his back. Over $50 million in cash and assets had been seized, and Mackey's operations in Atlanta, Nashville, and New Orleans were systematically dismantled. Everything Gordo had worked for was gone.

But one prize remained untouched: Michael LeCare's Colombian account for Michelle. Gordo didn't know how much money it contained, but he was sure it held the bulk of LeCare's savings. That account was his target, the key to rebuilding his life.

Gordo had learned of Becky and Michelle's escape to Bogotá through Mackey's private pilot. He didn't need a map to determine their destination—LeCare's penthouse apartment was the logical hiding place.

Adjusting the pistol tucked beneath his jacket, Gordo sat at a café across the street from the penthouse. The aroma of strong coffee mingled with the distant hum of traffic. He would wait. And when the moment came, he would strike with precision. This was his chance to reclaim everything he'd lost—and he wouldn't let it slip away.

Chapter 4:
Zipaquirá

Noon, Monday, Jan. 5, 1981

Becky and Michelle had two hours to explore the historic colonial town of Zipaquirá before touring the Salt Cathedral. The brick streets, lined with brightly colored buildings, gave the town an inviting and timeless charm, but Jose's warning about the man in a white suit dampened their enthusiasm.

"I'm trying to enjoy myself because this town is so different from Bogotá," Becky said, scanning the plaza. "But maybe we should eat lunch and take pictures on the way to the cathedral. I'd feel better once we're with a group."

"It's past twelve, and I'm hungry," Michelle replied. "Let's find a small café and order something. Nobody is going to bother us inside. Then we can decide what to do."

Becky nodded. They looked around and spotted a rustic sign that read *Casa Del Chorro*.

"Jose said all the restaurants around the plaza are pretty good. Let's try this place," Becky said as she looked around nervously.

The café's interior was warm and inviting, with dark wooden tables and walls adorned with local art. They chose a table near the window to see the plaza and keep an eye on the street.

A young waiter approached. His confident demeanor and polished English immediately set them at ease.

"My name is Roberto. May I get you something to drink first?"

"Two Colombian coffees," Michelle said, flashing a polite smile.

After Roberto left, Becky leaned forward and lowered her voice. "Do you think it was Gordo who followed us here?"

Michelle gulped. "I don't know. It seems someone might be."

"This morning, I started thinking about Jamaica, about that night, and now, Gordo could be here," Becky said. "I've been worrying he might show up one day."

Michelle glanced at Becky, shaking her head. "I've been worrying, too, especially when I feel like someone's watching us. I hate to say it, but part of me feels like we're still running."

Becky sighed, staring out the window. "Do you think we'll ever stop running? Maybe we should go back to Sarasota. Face whatever comes."

Michelle hesitated, her eyes narrowing. "We always knew we would, eventually. We haven't returned yet because we were worried he might be waiting for us, but if he is here and finds us..."

Her voice trailed off as Roberto returned with their coffees. "Gracias," said Michelle, waiting for him to leave.

"I was thinking. Miguel recommended we hire a bodyguard when we go places, just in case something like this happened," Michelle said. "What do you think? Michael hired a security company to watch the condo. Maybe one of the guards would help. They seem friendly and helpful."

Becky sipped the rich, dark brew, letting the bold flavor ground her thoughts. "Let's talk with Miguel when we get back. Having a bodyguard or two would be nice. But what about Sarasota? It's home, and I miss it. I miss feeling normal."

"I miss it, too," Michelle admitted as she sipped. "But it's not the same Sarasota we left. We'd have to worry about people looking for us there—Gordo, the DEA, and others we don't even know."

Roberto returned with steaming bowls of *ajiaco* soup.

"May I get you anything else, señoritas?" Roberto asked, his friendly tone breaking the tension at the table.

"No, thanks. We want to finish this. We've got some sightseeing to do before we leave town," Michelle replied.

They ate in silence, the warmth of the soup offering a fleeting comfort. But the unease lingered. Every few minutes, one of them would glance at the door or scan the other tables, searching for anything—or anyone—out of place.

Finally, Michelle spoke. "If we return to Sarasota, we probably would have to hire bodyguards. We can't be sure we are safe until Gordo is out of the picture. He won't stop, Becky. You know that."

Becky nodded slowly, her appetite fading. "I know. He always scared me, and now, knowing Robert hired him as an enforcer for his cocaine business, I'm even more frightened of him. But I hate living like this."

Michelle reached across the table and placed a hand on Becky's. "We'll figure it out. We've made it this far. And if we go back—when we go back—it'll be with a good plan."

Becky managed a faint smile. "Okay. But for now, let's try to enjoy this town and forget worrying about whether it's Gordo in the white suit or another tourist. For at least a couple of hours. I want to feel normal for a change."

Michelle squeezed her hand before pulling away. "Deal. Let's finish up and go for a walk. We can stay close to groups. If we're going to keep running, we might as well have some good memories along the way."

Roberto returned to check on their progress.

"How was your meal? Can I get you something else?" he asked.

"No, we're finished—just our check," Michelle replied. "After we walk around the plaza, what is the quickest way to the cathedral?"

"When you exit, take a right, and you will see the plaza. It's a short walk. Then, you can return the same way, go past Habla, and head to the salt mine," Roberto explained, placing the check between the two Americans.

"This is what our taxi driver suggested," Becky said. "Is it a 20-minute walk to the Salt Cathedral?"

"Sí, you will see street signs guiding you there," Roberto confirmed.

"Thank you, you've been very kind," Becky said.

Roberto nodded and left. Michelle left 150 pesos for lunch, plus a tip. The women stood up and left.

Becky and Michelle reached the plaza and looked around for anyone watching them. Then they saw the church. It was one of the most beautiful they had ever seen.

"Let's take some pictures," said Becky, asking a fellow tourist to capture a photo of her and Michelle in front of the impressive, tan stone façade of the Catholic Church.

They felt uneasy despite their agreement not to worry about

the man in the white suit. They couldn't shake the unsettling feeling of being followed while wandering the square, admiring local art and shop displays, and chatting with fellow tourists.

From a distance, Gordo watched Becky and Michelle with a smirk. As the women enjoyed lunch, he had changed from his trademark white suit to blend in with the tourist crowd.

He relished knowing they had no clue he'd been watching them the whole time. As they walked toward the Salt Cathedral, he felt a sense of triumph, amused by how easily he had outsmarted them. Now, he had to wait until they were alone to make his move.

Chapter 5:
The Salt Cathedral

1:50 p.m., Monday, Jan. 5, 1981

After a brisk and challenging walk uphill, they arrived at the entrance of the famed Salt Cathedral of Zipaquirá. Tall trees partially obscured it, but they saw the walkway leading to the tunnel entrance.

At the front gate, they presented their tickets to the attendant and were told to go inside. Their guide would meet them shortly, and the tour would start promptly at 2 p.m.

Becky and Michelle walked inside the mine. The brightness outside was met with the darkness inside, and it took a minute for their eyes to adjust.

"Do you hear those eerie sounds?" Michelle asked.

"Yes. It sounds like religious chanting," said Becky.

The chanting seemed to surround the two American ladies,

making what lay ahead a strange mystery. It beckoned them onward.

A few minutes later, the tour group leader appeared. In a loud voice, he told them his name was Jorge Posada and that he was happy they had chosen to visit the Salt Cathedral.

"Let me do a head count before we begin. My list says we have 15 people signed up for the two o'clock tour."

Jorge quickly counted. "Yes, yes, we have 15. Now that everyone is here, one more important thing. Please do not stray away from the group. If you wish to go alone, please let me know. I need to have an exact count at the end. I will keep a close eye on everyone during the tour. We do not want anyone to get lost down here," he said with a smile.

"Now, let me start by saying that as we walk through the tunnels to the cathedral, you will see wall carvings of the Stations of the Cross. They represent the 14 stages of Jesus's crucifixion," said Jorge solemnly. "They serve as a focal point for prayer and reflection, especially during Lent and the Holy Week of Easter."

Michelle whispered, "Becky, are you familiar with the Stations of the Cross?"

"A little. I went to a Catholic Church for a wedding. They had these stations with crosses on either side of the church's walls. These figures are very different because they are carved out of salt rock instead of the wood, stone, or metal used in the church," Becky said.

After a few minutes in the mine, Jorge described the first Station of the Cross.

"This is where Pontius Pilate condemns Jesus to death. He wanted to show mercy, but the chief priests shouted, 'Crucify him,' and he bowed to their pressure," Jorge said.

Next to the station was a small chapel with a lighted cross at the altar. "Anyone who wishes, we will stay to pray or meditate for a minute or two," he said.

After several people finished, the group continued their march downward. Jorge explained how the salt deposits were formed 250 million years ago and were raised above sea level when the Andes were formed.

He said men had mined the salt for decades, extracting its valuable mineral wealth, long before the Salt Cathedral was built in 1950. It was a tribute to human ingenuity and spiritual devotion.

"Some of you may be asking: why build these stations, this cathedral, so deep in the mountain?

"In 1932, miners built it as a place for daily prayers before starting work. They asked for protection from the saints. As time passed, safety concerns arose, so the government built the much larger New Salt Cathedral, which opened in 1954."

Jorge described each of the other 13 stations as they passed: when Jesus carried the cross, when he fell from injury and exhaustion, when he saw his mother, when he was crucified, and when he was finally laid to rest in his tomb.

"Michelle," Becky whispered. "I feel tingly. How do you feel?"

"I'm okay. Why?"

"Listening to Jorge talk, the deeper we go into the mine, the more I feel these waves of emotion coursing through me," Becky said, her voice animated and filled with excitement.

"Do you want to sit down and catch your breath?" Michelle asked, concerned.

"No, I want to keep going," Becky replied, her eyes sparkling enthusiastically. "It's a good feeling—almost like a rush of energy, a tingling feeling. Isn't it incredible how vast these tunnels are? How deep do they go? We've been walking for over an hour, and I love every moment of it. I feel alive and part of something bigger than myself."

"Me, too. I'm glad we came," Michelle said. "How do you feel? Still have that tingling feeling?"

Becky smiled. "I've felt that way before, but not 600 feet inside a salt mine," she said, laughing. "I feel fine now."

"I feel better, too," said Michelle. "I'm not as worried down here as I was when we were walking around town. I'm glad we came here."

Just then, Jorge announced they were nearing the end of the trail, where the main sanctuary of the Salt Cathedral stood. It was in a cavernous space with a giant, lighted cross at the altar and rows of pews where people sat.

As they approached, strains of "Ave Maria" filled the air, reminding visitors of the place's sacredness.

"Wow, look at the size of that cross!" Becky exclaimed. "It is huge, just like Jose said."

The group could see the giant cross illuminated by a purple light. The salt walls surrounding the cathedral glowed in blue, purple, and white lights. Everything in the room seemed to glisten in an otherworldly way.

"Masses are still held here," said Jorge. "It is quite inspiring when the church is full, and everyone is praying and singing."

Jorge led them to the pews. "This is the end of our tour. We will stay here for about 15 minutes. You may sit in the pews, pray, or contemplate what you've seen. I will be here to answer any questions. When it is time, I will lead us out."

Becky and Michelle sat down on a pew. They had walked many miles, but it was worth it. They felt renewed and awed by the sights they had seen.

"I have to say, I have new respect and understanding for what Jesus must have gone through after he was condemned. The pain and suffering he endured," Becky said.

"I never thought about it much. I knew Jesus died on the cross, but the hours leading up to that must have been brutal," Michelle said.

The two women sat in the pew without talking for another five minutes. When it was time to leave, Jorge said a few concluding words, and they walked with the group toward the exit.

"I am glad we are all still together. I hope you had as much fun as I did. Thank you for coming," said Jorge, counting the 15 visitors.

Becky and Michelle exited the mine a little after 4 p.m. and walked toward the taxi stand area to look for Jose.

However, Jose was nowhere to be found.

Chapter 6:
The Missing Taxi Driver

4:15 p.m., Monday, Jan. 5, 1981

An hour earlier, Jose had pulled his aging sedan into the taxi waiting area a block from the Salt Cathedral, muttering about the spare tire he had just replaced.

He had rushed back to the cathedral to pick up Becky and Michelle, and he felt lucky to arrive with plenty of time to spare. He had planned to take a few more fares in the city, but now he just wanted to rest, read a newspaper, and wait.

He was sitting in his car, reading his paper, when Gordo walked up.

"Taxi? Amigo, can you make a short run for me? I'm late for an appointment," Gordo asked pleasantly in Spanish.

"I've got a fare coming," Jose replied as he continued to

look at his paper. "Sorry, maybe another cab?"

"I'll pay you well," Gordo said, showing him a $20 bill.

Jose looked over and immediately recognized the man in the white suit and hat. *What should I do?* he wondered.

"I'm sorry, I can't," said Jose, his voice cracking nervously.

"It's just a few miles away," Gordo insisted. "Fifteen minutes, and you'll be back."

Jose checked his watch. It was 3:15 p.m. He had time, but something was wrong with this man. If he was the same man who had followed the two American women to town, what did he want now?

"You will take me," Gordo growled as he opened the back door and slid in.

Jose reached for the door handle of the taxi to get out, but he was slower than Gordo, who gripped the back of Jose's neck tightly.

"What—" Jose began, his voice cut off as Gordo yanked him backward, pressing him firmly against the seat.

Without hesitation, Gordo flicked open a switchblade with a sharp metallic click. In one swift motion, he slashed the razor-sharp blade across Jose's throat—severing arteries and flesh brutally.

Jose's eyes widened in shock and terror, a gurgling sound emanating from his lips as blood sprayed across the car's interior. His hands instinctively clawed at his neck, but it was futile.

Within seconds, Jose lost consciousness, his body slumping over lifelessly onto the front seat. Gordo calmly wiped the blade on Jose's shirt.

"I'm sorry, amigo," Gordo said, his voice low and mocking. "But I can't have you interfering."

Gordo looked around. There were no witnesses. With an evil grin, he exited the taxi and calmly walked to the cathedral's entrance.

*　*　*

Becky and Michelle found a bank of phone booths near the Salt Cathedral. Becky fumbled with the coins as she dialed Maria's number.

"Maria? It's Becky. Jose hasn't shown up, and we're getting worried. He told us about a man who might be following us to Zipaquirá, but now Jose isn't here. Have you heard from him?"

Maria's voice was tense. "He called earlier about a flat tire, but said he'd still make it. I haven't heard from him since. Stay where you are, and don't take a random taxi. If he doesn't show up soon, take the bus. Please be careful."

Becky hung up and turned to Michelle. "Maria said a flat tire might've delayed him. She said to take the bus if he doesn't show up."

Michelle nodded, glancing nervously around the bus stop. "I don't like this," she said.

"We don't have much time," Becky said. "Let's see if we can get two seats on that bus. I don't want to wait around if Gordo is following us."

There were several buses, but only one had "Bogotá" on the front. It was an old, aging bus with faded, vibrant paint and intricate designs.

"Pardon me, señor. Our taxi broke down. Do you have two seats for us?" Becky asked.

"Sí, we have two seats, but they are not together," the bus driver said.

"We'll take them. How much?" Becky asked.

"That will be 400 pesos for two tickets," the driver said.

Although Becky thought the price was extremely high, she did not want to quibble over it. She opened her purse and paid the driver. Michelle climbed into the bus cab.

Gordo saw the women boarding the bus. His jaw tightened. He was about to lose them again—a whole day wasted. As the bus pulled away a few minutes later, Gordo cursed as he watched it disappear down the road. Walking to his rented car, he promised that next time, they wouldn't be so lucky.

Chapter 7:
The Bus Ride Home

4:30 p.m., Monday, Jan. 5, 1982

Becky glanced back at the passengers. The bus was full of people—young and old, couples and families with children, commuters, workers, and tourists like themselves.

Four men were sitting together in the middle of the vehicle. They watched as Becky and Michelle bought their tickets and scanned the bus nervously for open seats.

One of the men, a heavyset American with curly brown hair, came forward, followed by another.

"Hello, miss. Can we help you get seats together?" the man said in a Southern American accent.

"Why, thank you," said Becky with a smile. "We have been sightseeing all day, and our taxi driver's car broke down. We are worried about getting home."

"No problem. Let us take care of it," said the man. "By the way, my name is Steve. I'm from Atlanta. This is Alejandro. He is from Colombia. We work together."

"Glad to meet you. I'm Becky, and this is Michelle."

"Hello to you both. Now, give us a few moments," Steve said.

While waiting for seats, Michelle whispered, "Do you think Jose's okay?"

"I hope so," Becky said with a frown. "But something tells me we must return to Bogotá as fast as possible."

Steve asked Alejandro in Spanish to arrange for some nearby passengers to switch seats with the empty ones in the back.

"Here you are, ladies. Take these seats in front of us," said Steve, who introduced them to Roger and Diego, two other co-workers who sat in seats to their left.

"I hope you like your seats. This bus isn't a Greyhound, but it usually gets from point A to B," Steve said with a grin.

"Thank you so much. You are all very kind. My Spanish is not as expert as yours," Michelle said.

"How lucky we are to have run into you," said Becky. "How is it you are on the bus?"

"We all work for a coal company based in West Virginia. We decided to take the day off and relax in Zipaquirá," Steve said.

"We walked through town before we went to the Salt Cathedral. It is lovely," Becky said.

"We've been there twice," said Steve with a smile. "Today, we just went into town for lunch and drinks and to buy presents for our families."

"How long have you been in Colombia?" Becky asked.

"This time, three months. Roger and I rotate in and out every six months with another team. Of course, Alejandro and Diego live here year-round, but they visit the States occasionally," Steve said.

"By the way, thanks again for helping. I was so worried when we couldn't find our taxi. It's been a long day," Michelle said.

"It's no problem. Steve is the boss. What he says, we do," chuckled Roger, a tall, lanky man with a Southern accent similar to Steve's.

"It is very unusual for us to get time off from work to go sightseeing. It just so happens that our workers went on strike last week. We aren't involved in the labor discussions, so we took a short vacation until it is resolved," Steve said.

"What company do you work for?" Michelle asked.

"Dagmire Energy. It's a U.S.-based coal company. We partner with a local Colombian company. It works out, usually. We have to negotiate with the unions every once in a while," Steve said. "Bad timing for Roger and me because it happened while we were here."

"Will it be a difficult negotiation?" Michelle asked.

"We hope not. The workers are paid fairly now. The problem is that an outside group is stirring them up. We don't know who is supporting them, so negotiations could take longer than usual," Roger said. "I stay out of that."

"What do you do for your company?" Michelle asked.

"Steve and I are mining engineers, and we make sure everything runs smoothly with the equipment and the mine. When it is closed, we have nothing to do," he said.

"What brings you two to Colombia?" Steve asked.

"Oh, it's a long story. We are just enjoying a little time away from Florida, where we lived before," Becky said.

"This is quite different than Florida, with the mountains and no beaches," Steve said. "Do you like it here?"

"I like it because it is different. For me, it's like an extended vacation. I am sure we will return to the States eventually," said Becky, trying not to give away too much information.

"I'm solely here for work. In a couple of years, my company will promote me, and I'll be working exclusively in mines in the U.S.," he said. "Frankly, I love Colombia, but the drug cartels are getting worse all the time. They are getting involved in many more things than drugs."

"What do you mean?" Becky asked.

"We don't know for sure, but we are concerned they might be assisting the union representing our workers," he said. "That could cause problems."

"Yes, I can understand that. We've been here five months and feel safe in Bogotá, but we haven't been outside the city too often," Becky said. "To tell you the truth, I hesitated to come to Zipaquirá because of the cartel violence we've heard about from our apartment manager. It hasn't affected us so far, but I worry."

Suddenly, the bus jolted to a stop, the screech of brakes echoing in the quiet countryside. The passengers exchanged worried glances.

Becky gripped the seat in front of her. "What's happening?" she asked nervously.

Michelle leaned forward, trying to peer out the windshield. "I don't know," she murmured.

"Todos permanezcan sentados (Everyone stay seated)," said the driver loudly in Spanish.

"¿Quiénes son esos hombres? (Who are those men?)" said someone in the back.

Becky turned to the window. Through the glass, she saw a group of men emerge from the brush lining the road. Her breath hitched.

"Oh my God," she whispered, her hand flying to her mouth.

At least fifteen were dressed in dark green paramilitary uniforms, their faces obscured by masks. The glint of sunlight off their automatic rifles made Becky's stomach churn.

The bus driver stood, his voice trembling as he addressed the passengers. "Permanezca sentado. No hagas movimientos bruscos. (Stay seated. Don't make any sudden moves.)"

"¿Quiénes son? (Who are they?)" a man near the front asked, his voice tinged with panic. "¿Qué quieren? (What do they want?)"

Steve, sitting across the aisle, leaned toward Becky and Michelle. His face was pale but determined. "Bandits," he said. "Probably cartel. Just do what they say. They probably only want our money and valuables."

A large, bearded man without a mask, in a dark green paramilitary outfit and a black beret, climbed the bus stairs. He was followed by another much smaller man wearing the same outfit.

"Pardon us, señors and señoritas," the large man said in a deep, gravelly Colombian accent. "We are here on Cali business. Cooperate, and no harm will come to you."

"You have obligations to us starting now. If asked, you will go outside and answer our questions," the big man growled. "Stay calm. Do not try to resist, or it will be bad for all."

Becky's heart pounded as the man's gaze fell on her. She instinctively turned her head, staring at the floor.

The big man looked directly at Becky and Michelle. "You two. Yes, you ladies. Please step out. Stand up and walk out."

Becky looked up with a terrified expression. Her legs felt heavy as she tried to stand. Michelle's hand tightly gripped her arm, and Becky could see she was just as frightened.

"But why?" Becky stammered, looking directly at the big man. "We haven't done anything. We are Americans on holiday."

Steve leaned over and whispered. "Do as they say. We have no choice."

"You are right, señor. You have no choice. Anyone who does not obey us immediately will be killed," the leader said.

Becky and Michelle rose unsteadily, their movements slow and deliberate. As they entered the aisle, the big man gestured to Steve, Roger, Alejandro, and Diego.

"Now you, señor, also out with your friend next to you and the other two gentlemen here."

The six of them were herded off the bus into the diminishing sunlight at the end of the hot summer's day. Fear gripped Becky as the other gunmen encircled them with weapons pointed.

"Sepáralos (Separate them)," the leader barked in Spanish. His men moved quickly, pushing Becky and Michelle away from the others. Becky whimpered as Steve, Roger, Diego, and Alejandro were moved to the side.

"What are they doing?" Michelle whispered, her voice trembling.

"I don't know," Becky replied, her voice barely audible.

As the little man harshly questioned parents and children on the bus, two gunmen took photographs and collected names from the passengers. Cries and protests were met with the butt of a rifle to the chest, silencing any dissent.

Becky heard the frightening sounds. What was going on? Perhaps a passing motorist could see what was happening and report it?

But if the police showed up, would there be a shootout? These gunmen were not the type to surrender. She wasn't ready for another gunfight, having just escaped one in Jamaica.

A few feet away, an argument broke out among the gunmen guarding the captives—their voices, sharp and urgent, carried over the tense silence.

"Sabemos quiénes son (We know who they are)," one said. "Trabajan para Dagmire. Terminemos esto. (They work for Dagmire. Let's finish this.)"

Steve's face went pale. "Wait," he said quickly, switching to Spanish. "We can negotiate. We can talk to Dagmire or the union. Whatever you need, please tell us."

The big man's eyes narrowed. He gave a curt nod.

Quickly, automatic weapons erupted in loud bursts. The two Americans, Steve and Roger, and the two Colombians, Diego and Alejandro, crumpled to the ground—their lifeless bodies riddled with bullets.

Becky's knees buckled. "Oh, my God," she gasped, her voice barely audible.

Michelle released a gurgling sob, placing her hands across her face.

The leader turned to face the remaining captives. "Todos, tranquilícense (Everyone, calm yourselves)," he said coldly, the smell of gunfire lingering in the air. "Hemos terminado. Se acabó. Escucha con atención y vivirás. (We are done. It is over. Listen carefully, and you will live.)"

The captors exchanged sharp commands, eyeing the remaining families. The air thickened with dread as the next move became uncertain.

In Spanish, the big man said, "These men we came for are dead. This is what will happen next. You will tell the police it was Cali. If you say anything different, we will come looking for you and kill not just you but your families."

"Do you understand? Repeat this together: 'We understand. It was the Cali who did this," the leader said. "Now, say it."

In unison, the people repeated, "Lo entendemos. Fue el Cali el que lo hizo."

In a cold and commanding voice, the leader said in Spanish, "As insurance, we will take these children. If you keep your promise to blame Cali, the children will be returned unharmed in one week. But if anyone tells a different story, they will be killed, and each one of you will be killed like dogs."

Sobbing, the mothers and fathers had no choice. Although every fiber of their being wanted to fight back, they knew from experience in dealing with drug cartels that it was hopeless. The only chance they had to see their children again was to be quiet and obedient.

"Good. Now we will leave," said the leader in Spanish, motioning for several men to take the children.

Becky put her hand over her mouth as she saw the children and their parents in agony. Michelle shook her head in disbelief.

The two women glanced again at Steve, Roger, and the two Colombians as they lay on the ground, their arms, legs, and torsos twisted unnaturally. Becky stared with furious eyes at the gunmen, wondering if they were finished with their violence.

The leader turned to the passengers and made one final, chilling threat. "Remember, there will be no second chances," the big man said in Spanish.

The air hung heavy with fear as the survivors grappled with the terror of what had just occurred.

As they left, the big man approached Becky, his dark eyes studying her. "Go, Becky Kendall," he said in English, his tone unnervingly calm.

Becky stared at him disbelievingly. "How do you know my name?" she whispered hoarsely.

He looked directly at her again and added, "Be safe. You are being watched."

Then he turned and walked away, leaving Becky stunned with fear and confusion. Michelle crawled over and said in a shaky voice, "What did he say?"

Becky began to cry. "He knows my name. He said I'm being watched."

Michelle shook her head. "What does he mean? Gordo?"

Just then, the bus driver sadly announced in Spanish, "Everyone, back on the bus. We're leaving."

Becky and Michelle took one more look at the lifeless bodies of their new friends.

In a trembling voice, Becky said, "We need to talk. But not here."

They boarded the bus in silence and took their seats.

Chapter 8:
Shaken but Alive

7 p.m., Monday, July 5, 1981

After a few minutes, Becky broke the silence. "What just happened?"

"I'm not sure," Michelle quietly replied. "Miguel told me about right-wing paramilitary groups and how they fight among themselves for power. This may be part of the battle."

"Why do you think they insisted they were the Cali cartel?" Becky asked. "What difference did that make?"

"I thought the same. It seemed this group wanted to blame Cali. They must have been Medellín and wanted to misdirect the police."

"But why did they kill Steve? And Roger? And those two Colombians?" Becky asked.

"I don't know," Michelle said. "What do you think?"

"Steve did say they were taking a few days off while their company settled labor union problems. He was worried the drug cartels might be getting involved in union affairs. I don't know why that is Medellín's business," Becky said.

"I'll ask Miguel when we get back," Michelle said. "He usually knows about these things."

Becky felt the parents' raw emotion as she heard their cries. She thought back to what the big man had told her.

"Michelle, I think the big man was strangely trying to protect us."

"He knew who you were. I don't know who those murderers work for, but they think someone is watching us," Michelle said. "It could be Gordo or the same person who followed us to Zipaquirá, as Jose thought."

"I thought he meant Gordo too," Becky said, briefly closing her eyes before adding, "But how would the big guy know my name?"

"Maybe through Robert?" Michelle said, her eyes darting. "Wait, now I remember: Michael once told me that Robert gets his cocaine from a man named Pablo Escobar. That's why Michael bought the condo in Bogotá—to do business here."

"Escobar? Isn't he the head of Medellín?" Becky asked.

"Yes. These gunmen must be Medellín, working for Pablo Escobar," Michelle said. "That is why they told us to say they were Cali. They are trying to shift the blame for what happened to their enemy. It's the only possible explanation."

"Escobar must be protecting us for some strange reason," she added.

"The big man warned us to be careful and said that someone was watching us. Do you think Escobar could be protecting us from Gordo?" Becky asked with a puzzled expression.

"Could be. Jose warned us about a man in a white suit, but we never noticed anyone. Now, the big man warned us.

I don't know, but we must be more cautious from now on," Michelle said.

Becky touched Michelle's arm and said, "I want to talk with you about Jamaica again."

"Are you sure? Remember how that would make us upset?" Michelle asked.

"Yes, but what just happened and worrying about Gordo brought it all back. I still can't get over how we managed to survive that month in Jamaica. It still feels like a nightmare," Becky said. "If we hadn't made it out, I keep wondering what would've happened to us."

"We did make it out," Michelle said firmly. "What bothers me is how wrong I was about Michael. He was involved in things like today."

"I had no idea Michael was involved in cocaine trafficking when I went to work for him at the High Seas Restaurant," Becky said.

"I should have told you more about Michael and Robert's business as soon as I found out," Michelle said. "It was a mistake. I didn't want to upset you."

"It wasn't your fault I went to Jamaica. Robert lied to me about having a nice two-week vacation. He told me I could go home anytime I wanted. Once I got there, he kept telling me I could go home after the political problems calmed down," Becky said.

"Michael told me the same," Michelle said.

"Little did I know Robert was an international cocaine trafficker, and he was waiting to make that one last coke deal. You didn't know until we got there," Becky said. "I knew something was off after the third day."

"I remember. I felt the same. Despite how Michael lied to

me all along, he came through by letting us out through that underground tunnel just before that big battle," Michelle said.

"You're right. For all Michael's faults, he came through in the end. I don't know how we would have survived if we had stayed in the big house," Becky said. "I was so scared hearing the gunfire as we were going down into the basement and then walking through that tunnel. He said a driver would take us to the plane, but I didn't think we would make it out."

"I felt the same. The explosions and gunshots were so loud that we could barely climb the ladder to the surface. All that noise, the screams... It was horrifying," Michelle said.

"We were so lucky to escape. I still hear the gunshot sounds in my head at night and sometimes in the morning when I wake up," Becky said.

"Me too. It's hard to shake it off. I keep thinking about how close we were to not making it out," Michelle said.

"Those memories are awful," Becky said.

"This is why we stopped talking about it in October. They did this to us. We didn't ask for any of it," Michelle said.

"Oh, I'm not so sure. I didn't know it, but I was part of that world when I bought and used cocaine. Jack told me to stop using so much. I didn't think it was hurting anyone, but now I know it was hurting me," Becky said.

"At least you had Jack. He looked out for you," said Michelle. "I had Michael, and he didn't care how much cocaine I used. He would have said something if he truly loved me like Jack loved you."

"He did, didn't he? And he was right," Becky said. "I was out of control. Oh, Michelle, I made so many bad choices when using."

Becky teared up, covered her face with her hands, and

then turned to Michelle.

"One night, when we were arguing, Jack told me I was turning into a junkie. I didn't believe it. He saw me changing, and I denied it. I was so mad at him, but he was right. I can't ever use drugs again."

"At least we stopped, and we got out. We must remind ourselves of that, even when it feels overwhelming," Michelle said.

"I am so thankful we have each other to lean on. I don't have Jack right now, but I do have you," said Becky, holding Michelle's hand.

"We'll get through this together, no matter how hard it gets," Michelle said.

"It is hard, but talking helps, even if it brings painful memories," Becky said.

"One day, it'll just be a bad memory, not a nightmare," Michelle said.

The two women looked at each other, holding hands. Tears ran down their cheeks, but they felt comforted knowing each felt the same. They had been through much more than anyone deserved.

"I just want to go home, get into bed, and sleep," said Becky as she turned to look out the window in the darkening sky.

"Me too. I want to close my eyes and pretend this never happened," Michelle said.

Despite the bouncy drive because of the old tires and uneven road, the next 15 minutes were quiet.

As they neared Bogotá, a line of police cars with blue lights flashing approached them at high speed. The bus driver pulled over. He got out to talk with what looked to be a captain.

After a minute, three police cars rushed to the location

where the bodies were found. It seemed someone had reported the crimes, prompting a response from the police.

The police seemed to understand what had happened without any explanation from the passengers. It was just another chapter in Colombia's ongoing drug and civil war, marked by violence and kidnappings in rural towns and along highways.

Chapter 9:
Making a Decision

10 a.m., Tuesday, Jan. 6, 1981

Even though she had a sleepless night, Becky kept to her routine and awoke earlier than Michelle.

As she entered the kitchen to make coffee, she wondered if there would be any news about the terrorist attack and the killing of the four men on the bus from the Salt Cathedral in Zipaquirá.

After returning to Bogotá, the police questioned everyone on the bus. Becky and Michelle stuck to the story about the Cali gunmen. They acknowledged speaking to Steve and Roger on the bus. They told police that the men helped get them seats and said they worked for Dagmire Energy.

"Good morning. How did you sleep?" said Michelle as she walked on the balcony.

"Terrible dreams," Becky said.

"I didn't sleep so well, either. I thought a day trip would be fun," Michelle said.

"I thought so too. When we were driving out to Zipaquirá, Jose told us about the Andes Mountains, the quiet villages, and the beautiful scenery, and I thought we should get out of Bogotá more," Becky said.

"But now, I just want to hide in our apartment for the next week," she added.

"I was thinking the same. The Salt Cathedral was amazing, and Zipaquirá was beautiful. I wish we had spent the night in the town after Jose's car broke down, but I was bothered by the American he thought was following us," Michelle said. "Do you still think it was Gordo?"

"I have a strong feeling it was, but we didn't see anyone in a white suit or anyone who looked like him, even though the big man told us someone was watching us," Becky said, shivering at the thought.

"If it were him, I'm not sure staying the night would have been better," Michelle said. "We would have missed that bus, but it could have been worse."

Becky nodded. "The whole day was strange. At least we got home."

Suddenly, a loud explosion shook their condominium. Three streets away, they saw a large building explode, with bricks and debris flying into the air. The building became engulfed in flames, and smoke billowed into the clear, blue morning sky.

Startled, Becky jumped to her feet and stood beside Michelle.

"Oh my God!" Becky exclaimed. "What is it?"

"I don't know. It could be a terrorist attack. Look at that fireball!"

"Isn't that the big federal building downtown?" Becky asked.

"Yes, I think so," said Michelle.

"Who would do that?" Becky asked.

"That's not Cali or Medellín. Probably FARC," Michelle said.

"FARC?" asked Becky.

"FARC is the Revolutionary Armed Forces of Colombia, a Marxist communist group. They have been waging war against the government for 30 years. They are just a bunch of terrorists," she said.

"Another gang? This is getting too much," Becky said in disbelief as she stared at the rising smoke. She heard fire truck sirens go off in the distance.

"Miguel told me they are involved in kidnappings and drug trafficking, like Cali and Medellín," Michelle said. "They are getting more daring and targeting government buildings closer to the city. That's another reason we must be more careful on the streets."

Becky could only stare at the burning building, with smoke rising into the sky and sirens filling the air.

"I didn't want to worry you about everything that was going on between FARC, the drug cartels, and the government," Michelle said. "These bombings are getting worse."

"And closer. I've heard you talk about it a little with Miguel," Becky said. "Michelle, Miguel said we'd be safe downtown, but I am not so sure now, with a bombing right in our neighborhood and what happened on the bus last night."

"He always warns us to be careful," said Michelle as she stared at the scene.

"We should ask Miguel about the bodyguards today," Michelle added.

"Yes," said Becky, who suddenly made a decision she'd been considering for the past two months: "Michelle, listen to me. We talked about this yesterday. It's time we go home."

Michelle turned toward her. "Yes, it's time. It's been nice relaxing here at Michael's safe house, but with last night and this, five months is enough. This place has become too dangerous. We need to move on with our lives."

"I'm glad we agree," Becky said. "Let's do it."

"I've been thinking about this. I still have my house in Sarasota. You can live with me until you make other arrangements," Michelle said.

"I miss Sarasota. It's the best place for us now," said Becky, still watching the smoke rise from the burning building.

"Let's go to the bank and transfer money to our accounts in Florida," Michelle said. "I am sure Miguel will watch over our place here, as he did before with Michael. We can keep it or sell it later."

"I should finish that letter to Jack and tell him we're coming. I don't want to show up and surprise him," said Becky. "I have to think more about what I want to tell him."

"You mean if you want to ask him to take you back?" Michelle asked.

"It would be more complicated than that, Michelle," Becky said.

Chapter 10:
The Letter

11 a.m., Tuesday, Jan. 6, 1981

Becky entered her bedroom, opened her top dresser drawer and took out her wedding picture with Jack. She set it on the table and stared at it.

She removed her pajamas and looked at her naked body in the mirror. She was tall with a sleek figure, full breasts, long wavy red hair, and soft white skin.

As she gazed at her reflection, she wondered: Who was she? What had she become? Could she go back to Jack? She missed him. She missed having a man, and Jack was still her husband.

She suddenly felt nervous. Thinking she was close to a decision about Jack, she shook her head and went into the bathroom to shower. She had things to do and decisions to make, including finishing the letter to Jack that she had started and stopped so many times.

$$* \quad * \quad *$$

Michelle shivered as she took off her clothes and stepped into the shower. As the warm water splashed on her face and body, thoughts flashed through her mind about returning to Sarasota. She missed the States, but not Florida so much.

She could sell her house in Sarasota, buy something in Chicago, or move to Mesa, where the Cubs trained. Or she could live in three places. She had enough money.

But she had grown close to Becky and wanted to ensure she was all right with Jack. She'd stay in Sarasota a while longer to see what happened.

Michael's money gave her many options. If only she could leave Bogotá; she now feared this place.

$$* \quad * \quad *$$

Becky stepped out of the shower, dried off, and walked into her bedroom with a towel wrapped around her body.

Her mind was on Jack. She had been thinking a lot about him while she was in Bogotá. He was always patient and understanding, except for her increasing cocaine use.

As she dried off, she looked at their wedding picture once again. He was tall, strong, and sharp in his tailored navy-blue suit; she appeared stunning in her low-cut white dress with detailed lace that highlighted her fiery red hair and striking blue eyes.

She remembered 1975, when she moved to Sarasota from Chicago on a lark. She just wanted warm winters and sandy beaches.

Becky had met Jack one evening at a popular downtown

restaurant where she was a server. He had come in with his newspaper friends. He flirted with her, and she felt a connection.

The next time he came in, she made it a point to catch his eye. He took the bait, asked her out, and they immediately became inseparable.

They dated for six months, and one night at a private dinner at Café Baci, he surprised her with a proposal.

She immediately blurted out a "yes" without giving it much thought. They had a big wedding, with her friends coming from Chicago and all his friends from Sarasota and Gainesville.

Her memories of Jack were strong. She didn't want to admit how much she loved him.

She reflected on the next four-plus years and how quickly they'd passed. They did everything together. Jack was lively, knew lots of people, and always had kind words about her. But as Becky's cocaine use grew, he began to act differently, at least from her perspective.

Even though she believed she was justified in taking a break from their marriage, she now knew it was a lie.

During her two weeks at Mackey's drug house, Becky realized she had fooled herself into believing she had left because she was tired of him questioning her increasing cocaine use and how she spent her savings.

She reflected on the last few letters to Jack while in Jamaica. In those letters, she had expressed that she was in danger and had pleaded with him to rescue her. He came and risked his life to save her.

*Please hurry. I don't know how much
longer I can last here. I've heard gunfire in*

the woods around the house. Robert says
people are just trying to scare us. It worked.
I'm scared and want to come home.

But Becky also regretted the letter she had written him after arriving in Bogotá, while he was waiting for her at GoldenEye. What was she thinking?

I thought long and hard about asking you
here. Sorry, but I decided I couldn't drag
you into this. I can't explain anymore
except to say I'm safe and very wealthy.

And what was even worse, she signed her last letter, "*Goodbye, Becky.*"

Of course, Michelle had just given her the $2.5 million; at the time, she thought that was all she needed. She shuddered when she thought of her state of mind when she wrote to Jack that they should go their separate ways. She still hadn't stopped using.

Months later, she knew that letter was a terrible mistake. First, it was the cocaine, then the money that had warped her thoughts and caused her to make bad decisions.

As she stood looking in her closet for clothes to wear, events, distance, and time made it clear that she had been out of control with her cocaine use and that she misunderstood the true meaning of marriage.

She also thought about how she had thrown away a rewarding and fun career in the restaurant business.

From the other room, Michelle called out. "How are you doing? Almost ready?"

"I still need to get dressed, and I want to look over the letter to Jack. Give me 15 minutes," Becky said.

"All right, but don't take more. I want to get to the bank," Michelle said.

As Becky put on her bra, underwear, and a vibrantly printed floral dress in bold tropical colors, she considered the final changes to her letter.

She walked to the kitchen to get another cup of cappuccino, returned to the bedroom, and sat by the window in her chaise lounge. As she sipped her warm drink, the words she wanted to say started to take shape in her mind.

Memories of Jack and her restaurant jobs flooded back. She scribbled a few more sentences and crossed out some others. After visiting the bank, she would rewrite the letter and mail it at the first opportunity.

She felt confident about her decision to return to Sarasota. She'd ask Jack to take her back.

Chapter 11:
Walk to the Bank

Noon, Tuesday, Jan. 6, 1981

Becky and Michelle descended the elevator and strode past the front desk in the building's lobby.

"Goodbye, Miguel, we'll be back in a few hours," Michelle said to Miguel Rodriguez, who managed the condo building where they lived.

"Take care, ladies," replied Miguel cheerfully.

"Oh, wait, I almost forgot. Becky and I were talking about hiring a bodyguard. Can you check into that for us with the security company?" Michelle asked.

"Because of last night?" Miguel inquired.

"Yes, and other things as well. We will talk with you when we get back," Becky said.

"Where are you going in such a hurry?" Miguel asked.

"To the bank. We shouldn't be long," Becky said.

"Be watchful," Miguel said, waving goodbye.

As the two American women walked to the downtown

main branch office of the Banco Nacional, they chatted about finally going home.

"I'll get us plane tickets when we return to the apartment," Michelle said.

"First class," Becky said with a big smile. She was relieved to have made such a big decision. She felt happy for the first time in months.

"Of course," Michelle said with a laugh. "We can afford it."

After a 15-minute walk, Becky and Michelle entered the bank. Michelle asked to speak with an account executive who could authorize the wire transfer to Florida.

"Good morning, señoritas. What can I do for you?" said Juan Domingas, a pleasant-sounding young account executive.

"We'd like to close our accounts and transfer our balances to the United States," said Michelle.

"I can make that happen, but we will be sorry to see you go," Juan said. "Just give me your account information, show me your identification, and fill out these forms."

After showing Juan their identification and completing the necessary paperwork, Becky and Michelle each transferred nearly all the $2.5 million they had in their accounts to Sarasota.

"I am happy you decided not to close your accounts," Juan said. "Leaving $10,000 in your accounts was a wise choice. You may wish to return one day."

"You are right, Juan. Bogotá is a lovely city. We will come back at some point," said Michelle.

Chapter 12:
Gordo Intervenes

1 p.m., Tuesday, Jan. 6, 1981

As they exited the bank, they were discussing the ease of the wire transfer when Gordo approached them from behind.

"Becky Kendall. Well, well. After all this time, imagine seeing you in Bogotá. Keep walking, and don't say a word."

Becky and Michelle exchanged a glance before looking around to see if anyone nearby could help them. There wasn't. A few people were walking on the other side of the street, but none were in front of them for another block.

"We will walk back to your place very calmly. I will tell you what to do. If you scream, it will be your last breath."

"What do you want, Gordo?" Becky nervously asked.

"You'll find out soon enough," he said. "Shut up. Keep walking."

Becky realized now that Gordo had followed them to Zipaquirá, just as Jose thought, and he'd been the one watching them, as the big man had told her. She hesitated to ask, not wanting to make the situation worse.

Michelle hoped that when Miguel saw them enter the condo building with a stranger, he would alert the security team protecting their apartment so they could come to help.

But as they approached their building, Gordo ordered them to turn right into a street where he had parked his rental car.

Michelle realized they were in serious trouble. "Where are we going? We have at least $5,000 in our condo," she said. "You can have it."

"Keep walking," Gordo said. "Here we are. Get in the car."

The women stopped. Gordo poked Becky with the gun that was hidden under his newspaper. She flinched as she felt the steel barrel.

"Go on," said Gordo. "Both of you. Back seat."

Becky began to whimper. "Why? Where are you taking us?" she asked, trembling with fear.

"Stupid questions. You're not the boss's pet anymore. You aren't in Florida. Get in and don't cause any trouble," Gordo snarled.

The two women had no choice but to comply. As he slammed the door, Gordo added, "And your husband isn't here to save you."

Chapter 13:
No Way Out

1:30 p.m., Tuesday, Jan. 6, 1981

Gordo drove through the winding streets of Bogotá, the car's tires humming against the pavement. Becky and Michelle were in the backseat—and they were terrified.

Taking turns through less crowded areas, Gordo finally pulled to an old, abandoned warehouse on the city's outskirts. Surrounded by overgrown weeds and dilapidated fences, the building was tucked away from the main roads.

Gordo got out of the car and signaled for Becky and Michelle to walk ahead of him. They exchanged nervous glances before stopping at a side entrance. "Open it," he barked. The door creaked as they pushed through.

Inside, broken windows let slivers of sunlight filter through, dimly lighting the old warehouse. The heavy air was filled with dust and the faint smell of rust.

Gordo said nothing and led the women to a small room in the back. It was furnished with a rickety table and a few chairs. The oppressive silence was broken only by the distant sounds of the city and the occasional drip of water from a leaking pipe.

Gordo gestured to the chairs. "Sit down," he commanded harshly.

Becky and Michelle sat.

"What's he going to do?" Michelle whispered, on the verge of tears.

"I don't know," Becky replied, wondering what to do or say. "We must stay calm and find a way out of this."

Gordo's cold eyes, filled with cruel intent, bore down on them. Escape seemed impossible, and the terror of what might come next made every moment more unbearable.

"Now, you're going to tell me everything. What did you do with Robert's money?" he growled, his eyes narrowing.

"It's Michelle's. Michael gave it to her," Becky said.

"You lie. Where is it?" Gordo barked.

"We don't have it. We transferred it to our accounts in Florida," Becky said. "Please believe us. We decided this morning to leave."

Michelle interrupted. "I have bank receipts. Do you want to see them? Becky is telling the truth."

"Show me," he said.

"They're in my purse."

"Open it slowly," he said.

As Michelle handed him the receipts, Gordo's face contorted with rage. He slammed his fist on the table, causing the rickety furniture to shake.

"Do you think you can fool me? Do you think showing me these receipts will save you?" Gordo's voice was dangerously loud, and his eyes blazed with fury.

Becky and Michelle exchanged frightened glances, knowing they needed to tread carefully.

Gordo paced the small room, his anger simmering just below the surface. "You've wasted my time and my boss's money. There are consequences for that."

"Wait. I have $10,000 left in my account. I can get you that," Michelle said.

Gordo suddenly stopped and turned toward the women.

"I'll tell you what I want. Return to the bank and take all the money out of your accounts," said Gordo, looking at Michelle. His voice was now cold and calculating.

"The more you give me, the better your chance to live. If you don't come back with it in one hour, Becky will die, and you'll pay in other ways," said Gordo, his voice echoing with menace.

"Wait," he said as a thought passed through his mind. "Maybe it's not too late to have your wire transfer reversed if you did it in the first place. How much did you transfer?"

Michelle glanced at Becky, who nodded.

"Nearly $2.5 million," Michelle said.

"Good. Tell the bank you made a mistake. You want to stop the transfer and put it back into your account. Then, take out as much as you can in cash," said Gordo, his eyes gleaming.

He took a rope from the table and tied Becky's hands to the chair.

"No, Gordo! Stop!" Becky pleaded, tears running down her face. Gordo then gagged her.

"She will be waiting here with me. Take the car," he said, handing Michelle the keys. "Now go. Remember: one hour, or she dies."

Becky and Michelle locked eyes, their fear laced with silent determination.

Michelle, her heart pounding, rushed to the bank. The minutes ticked by in her mind like a countdown.

After parking, she calmed herself and entered the bank. She looked for Juan Domingas and saw him busy with another client. She had to wait.

The minutes felt like an eternity. Michelle tried to steady her breathing, but her anxiety kept creeping back. She thought about Becky, all tied up. How was she? Michelle realized everything was her own fault. What an idiot she'd been to encourage Becky to go to Jamaica and stay in Bogotá these past months. Then again, why did she rush to the bank before hiring the bodyguard?

She glanced at Juan. He was still talking with the other customer. She fiddled with the strap of her purse, her fingers tapping rhythmically against the leather, a nervous habit she couldn't break.

Finally, Juan was free and noticed her pacing nearby.

He approached her and asked kindly, "Señorita, is something wrong?"

"I made a mistake. Can I reverse some of the money I transferred this morning? I need to withdraw more and keep more in my account," Michelle nervously asked.

"I'm sorry, not for a week. The money transfer is already in process," Juan said.

"Oh, no. How much can I withdraw? We forgot to take some spending money. What can you do for me?" said Michelle in a desperate tone.

"I believe you have $10,000 in your account left. Just fill out this withdrawal slip. Are you sure you're all right? Where is your friend?" Juan asked.

"Uh, she is sick at home. I need more. Can I withdraw from her account as well?"

"No, I'm sorry. We need her direct authorization."

Michelle grimaced. She took the slip and began writing the $10,000 withdrawal.

Juan looked at the amount.

"This will close your account. Are you sure?"

"Yes, please do it," Michelle said.

Juan stood up and walked over to a cashier's window. "Isabella, will you make this withdrawal for me? Michelle Talley is closing her account," he said.

Juan walked back with the $10,000 in an envelope.

"Michelle, here is your money. Your account is now closed. But I am concerned. I sense something is wrong," Juan said.

"No, this will take care of it," said Michelle with a meek smile.

As she left the bank, Juan picked up the phone and called the police.

*   *   *

Michelle drove carefully back to the warehouse. She hoped Gordo would accept the $10,000 and let them go.

But when she arrived, Gordo's expression was angry and impatient.

"How much did you get me?"

With tears in her eyes, Michelle shook her head. "I could only withdraw $10,000. It was all I had. They refused to reverse the wire transfer or let me take any money from Becky's account."

Becky's face went pale as the weight of Michelle's words sank in. Her wide, tear-filled eyes darted to Michelle, who slowly handed Gordo the thick bank envelope.

Gordo opened it and thumbed through more than 500 1,000-peso bills, smiling sinisterly.

"Let me go back to our apartment. I have more than five thousand American dollars at home," Michelle pleaded. "Next week, we can get the money back from Sarasota."

He shook his head and turned to Becky, sitting in the corner of the room, her eyes wide with fear. He grabbed her by the arm, dragged her to the center of the room, and ripped off her gag.

"Do you have anything left to say?" Gordo snarled.

"Gordo, stop it!" Becky cried out in pain. "Listen to Michelle. We can get what you want."

Michelle rushed forward, trying to intervene. "Please, don't hurt her! I did what you asked!"

Gordo shoved Michelle back, his grip tightening on Becky. "You both think you can mess with me and get away with it?"

Becky winced as Gordo's grip became more painful. "Please," she whispered, voice trembling. "We can find another way to get you more money. Jack has it. He can give it to you. Let me call him. You know he will do it. Just give us more time."

"Jack *will* give it to me next time I see him," said Gordo. "Unfortunately, for you two, you're out of time."

He raised his Ruger MK and began firing.

Chapter 14:
Bad News

10 a.m., Friday, Jan. 9, 1981

Jack was sitting at his desk when the phone rang.

"*Herald-Tribune*. This is Jack."

"Jack Kendall?"

"Yes."

"I am Detective Matias Morales with the Bogotá Police Department," he said.

"Bogotá?" Jack repeated, surprised.

"Yes. I'm sorry. We have bad news," Morales said. "Please sit down."

"What is it, detective?"

"We regret to inform you that your wife, Becky Kendall, and her friend, Michelle Talley, have been murdered. We are very sorry," the detective said.

"What did you say?" Jack exclaimed.

"You should come to Bogotá, identify the bodies, and arrange their return. Call the American Embassy here and let them know you're coming. They know about the deaths."

"Go to Bogotá?" he replied, still not quite comprehending.

"Sí. You should come as soon as possible."

"Are you sure it's her? Maybe it's a mistake? Becky has been on vacation, that's all."

"No, it is not a mistake. We are sure. We found identification," the detective said.

"What happened?"

"I can't tell you much now. Your wife was shot. We are following up on leads. When you get to the main police station in Bogotá, ask for me. I will be able to tell you more. Again, I am very sorry. Please come," the detective said.

Jack took a deep breath and exhaled. "Yes, Detective Morales."

He placed the receiver down and stared off into space. Tears ran down his cheeks. He put his head on his desk and started to moan softly.

A low murmur arose among the reporters and editors in the newsroom who'd heard bits and pieces of the conversation and saw Jack slump over his desk. Bobbie Jackson, the paper's police reporter and one of Jack's closest friends, came over to check on him.

"Jack, what is it? What happened?" Bobbie asked soothingly.

"She's dead. Becky," was all Jack could say.

Bobbie froze in shock. Her eyes widened in disbelief. Becky, her longtime rival for Jack's affections, was dead?

"Let's go somewhere and talk," said Bobbie. "Let me help you up."

Jack slowly got up. His hands and feet tingled. His head felt light.

"Bobbie, she's gone. I never imagined I'd lose Becky like this or that I'd never see her again," he said.

"Who did you talk with?" Bobbie asked.

Jack could barely speak. He began to hyperventilate.

"Sit down for a minute. Take some deep breaths," Bobbie said.

"It was the detective. He wants me to call the embassy in Bogotá and make arrangements. I have to go to Bogotá!" Jack exclaimed.

"I can help. Please let me know what you would like me to do. I'll call the embassy," she said. "Let me take you home. You shouldn't have to bear this alone."

Jack staggered back, gripping the table's edge as though it might anchor him to the reality he couldn't yet comprehend.

"Jack, we'll get through this together," Bobbie said firmly, stepping closer.

He stared blankly at her. "She needed me, and I wasn't there. I should have stopped this."

"You couldn't have known," Bobbie said, her voice breaking but steady. "What matters now is what you do next."

Jack straightened, his grief turning into determination. "I'm going to Bogotá," he said firmly. "I'll find out who did this and make them pay."

Bobbie nodded, noticing the fire in his eyes. "Then we'll start making arrangements. Tonight."

Chapter 15:
Trip to Bogotá

7 a.m., Sunday, Jan. 11, 1981

Jack didn't speak much during the eight-hour trip from Sarasota.

It was incredibly ironic that Jack had tracked Becky to Jamaica six months earlier, only to lose her after the horrific gun battle on the mountain. Now, he was heading to Colombia to claim her body.

At least he wasn't alone; Bobbie, a trusted friend, sat beside him on the flight. He didn't know how he would've managed everything without her. He kept shifting between shock, disbelief, and anger.

At the Bogotá airport, they took a cab to Becky's condo. Jack wanted to meet with Miguel Rodriguez, Becky's apartment manager, to find out what he knew and see if they could stay there. If not, they'd find a hotel.

It was getting late in the day, and he didn't want to go to

the police station or morgue immediately.

"Will you be all right?" Bobbie asked. "I can talk with the manager if you want."

"No, I need to do it myself and find out what I can. Feel free to ask any questions."

Jack and Bobbie opened the front door of the condominium building. They saw a man sitting behind a desk by the elevator.

"I'm looking for Miguel Rodriguez. Are you him?" Jack asked.

"Sí, señor. What can I do for you?" Miguel asked.

"I'm Jack Kendall, Becky Kendall's husband."

"Ah, of course. Detective Morales told me you'd be coming. I'm so sorry about Becky and Michelle," Miguel said.

"Thank you. We want to stay in the apartment. Will that be all right?" Jack asked.

"Sí, show me identification, and I will give you the key," Miguel said.

Jack took out his passport and showed it to the manager. Miguel looked at it carefully and nodded his head.

"We have to be very careful. These are bad times in Bogotá. Your wife and Michelle were always kind and friendly to me. I miss them," Miguel said.

Jack nodded. "Thank you. I am still processing what happened. If you don't mind, could you answer a few questions?"

"I don't mind. I have been told that you are a journalist in Florida. I told the police I didn't see anything. I was inside the building."

Bobbie moved closer. "Hi, Miguel. I am Bobbie Jackson. Did you see them at all that morning?"

"Sí, the ladies left Tuesday morning, all dressed up. Despite what had happened the day before, they seemed happy. They said they were going to the bank and would be back shortly. They never returned. The police told me what happened," Miguel said.

Jack slumped, dropped his head, and asked, "What happened the day before?"

"There was a cartel attack on their bus coming back from Zipaquirá. Four Americans were killed. Detective Morales can tell you more about it," Miguel said. "He thought there might be a connection, as the cab driver who took them there was later found murdered."

Jack's eyes widened. "Murdered?"

"Sí. Ask the detective. I understand he was a family man, very religious," said Miguel, shaking his head. "I hate what is happening to my city."

Jack gritted his teeth. "Have you seen any strangers linger around here before or after?"

"Well, now that you mention it, I did tell the police there was one man," Miguel said.

"What did he look like?"

"American. He had a heavy black mustache, dark sunglasses, and a white suit. He might have been wearing a white hat," Miguel said.

"A white suit?"

"Sí, he stood across the street at the café for some time before the ladies walked out. I remembered him because he had been hanging around there several times before," Miguel said.

"And you told the police this?"

"Sí."

Jack froze as the description sank in—an American in a

white suit and hat. His jaw clenched, his breath quickened, and a low growl escaped his throat. Despite the half-assed disguise, it had to be Gordo. The bastard was here, in Bogotá.

He felt like someone had punched him in the gut. Gordo hadn't just been following Becky and Michelle; he'd been stalking them, waiting for the right moment to strike. A surge of rage boiled inside him, overpowering the sorrow that had gripped him since Becky's death. If Gordo were here, it wouldn't be a coincidence. Jack's fists tightened.

"Gordo," Jack hissed through clenched teeth. "That son of a bitch. He's the one. He killed her. He killed them both."

Bobbie watched Jack's reaction closely, her face full of worry.

"Jack, we aren't sure yet. We need to talk with the police to see if he's a suspect," Bobbie said. "It could be someone else."

"I doubt it, but you're right. I have to keep an open mind until we have evidence," said Jack, starting to make sense of what happened. "Miguel, we'll stay the night."

"Bueno. Here is the key. The apartment is on the fifth floor. Number 18, straight ahead off the elevator," he said.

After thanking Miguel, Jack and Bobbie got on the elevator. A few seconds later, the door opened. Jack hesitated.

"Jack, let's get this over with," Bobbie said.

He stepped out into the hall.

There it was, No. 18, just as Miguel said. Taking a deep breath, Jack walked toward the door, paused again, slid in the key, and opened it.

The penthouse suite's living room was well-furnished. Bobbie noticed how spacious and airy it was. Its open-plan layout seamlessly connected the living room, dining area, and kitchen.

A large, floor-to-ceiling sliding glass door led to what

appeared to be a balcony, offering a panoramic view of the distant Andean mountains and the bustling cityscape below.

They walked into the living room onto a beautiful Persian rug that overlaid the polished parquet floor. The room also featured plush, inviting, overstuffed sofas and armchairs upholstered in rich, earthy tones of deep reds and browns. A vintage coffee table crafted from dark mahogany wood sat in the center, adorned with intricate carvings.

Bobbie thought the furniture and paintings in the room were expensive. She wondered whether Becky and Michelle had bought them or if they had already been there when they arrived.

As Jack scanned the room, he looked for anything that could be Becky's. He walked past the kitchen to the large outside balcony with chairs and a table.

He froze when he saw what was on the table: Becky's reading glasses and her favorite book, *Sophie's Choice* by William Styron. How many times had she read it? It was almost like she was still here.

There was another book he didn't recognize, *I'm OK – You're OK*, by Thomas Anthony Harris. Was she searching for answers or trying to reassure herself?

A wave of grief swept over him, so intense it nearly buckled his knees. "Becky..." he whispered. The glasses, the books— they weren't just objects. They were pieces of her, fragments of a life now gone.

For the first time since arriving in Bogotá, the weight of her death crashed over him, suffocating and relentless. He sank into the nearest chair, clutching the glasses in his hand.

"I should've been here," he murmured as tears filled his eyes. "I should've protected you."

Bobbie's voice broke the moment. "Jack, come back here. It's the bedrooms," she called out from the living room.

Before he left, he picked up the well-worn book, looked inside for anything of hers, and then placed it down. He took a deep breath, trying to shake off his sorrow.

Down the hall, Bobbie was in the first bedroom. She stood there watching him as he entered.

In the middle was a king-sized bed with a carved wooden headboard and luxurious bedding in shades of cream and gold. A comfortable chaise lounge was by the window. Two American magazines were on a side table. A walk-in closet offered ample storage.

Then his breath caught. On the dresser, he saw a familiar memento: their wedding picture, framed in gold.

Jack sat on her bed, stared at the photo for several seconds, and then turned away.

"Why does she have this here?" Jack exclaimed.

"This must be a copy. You still have your original at home in your bedroom," Bobbie observed.

Jack said nothing. He sat on the bed, looking at the picture, and turned away a few moments later.

Bobbie became worried about the effect the picture was having on him. She knew how much he did to find Becky in Jamaica. Then, all in the name of money, Becky ran further away to Bogotá. She didn't understand Becky.

"I'll pack these personal things if you want," said Bobbie, hoping Jack would say no.

Jack nodded, but he had little to say. He couldn't leave her things in Bogotá and didn't want to throw them out.

As Bobbie went to look for some boxes, Jack stood up, walked over to Becky's writing desk, and opened the drawer.

It was filled with various papers, bills, statements, and odds and ends.

Then he saw a letter. He froze when he recognized Becky's handwriting.

"Bobbie, can you come and read this letter? I don't think I can. It's in Becky's handwriting," he said, sitting back on the bed.

Bobbie returned to the room, picked up the letter, and looked it over.

"What does it say?" Jack asked.

"Are you sure you don't want to read it yourself? It looks very personal," Bobbie said.

"No, just tell me," Jack insisted.

"This is an unfinished letter to you. You mentioned the last one you got was at GoldenEye in Jamaica, when she said goodbye. Is that right?" asked Bobbie.

"That was the last one," said Jack quietly as he sat on the bed.

"Hmm. She never mailed this one, then. There are lots of changes. Words and sentences crossed out, rewritten," she said. "Give me a minute."

Bobbie studied the page, frowning.

"This letter is confusing. Becky talked about coming back to Sarasota. Toward the end, she wrote about being scared of living here. Something about a trip to the Salt Cathedral, where men were killed on a bus," Bobbie said. "That's what Miguel mentioned."

"Go on," Jack said.

"She and her friend Michelle decided to leave Bogotá because of the terrorist bombings in the city," Bobbie said.

"She knew this was a dangerous place, just like Jamaica,"

he said. "Why did she come here?"

"I don't know," said Bobbie, glancing at him momentarily, then back to the letter. "She also talked about how she missed you and regretted staying away so long. She was worried about coming back and how it might affect you."

Bobbie paused. Jack was quiet.

"She didn't say directly, but I think it is safe to conclude she didn't come back sooner because of the money she had here," Bobbie said. "I am not clear what she meant by that. She kept on crossing out things. Didn't you tell me something about her coming into a lot of money?"

"Yeah, she told me not to worry about her because she was safe and very wealthy," Jack said. "I always wondered what she meant. What else did she say?"

"She finished the letter by crossing out and rewriting several sentences that seemed to say she wanted to see you again," Bobbie said. "It's hard to decipher because she replaced them with stronger statements about wanting to be your wife again if you wanted her back. She had trouble with the ending."

Bobbie took a breath. "Jack, she said she still loved you."

As he sat on Becky's bed, listening to Bobbie summarize his wife's last letter, he pictured Becky sitting at the writing table or possibly on the balcony, deciding whether to return to him.

It was surreal and bittersweet to learn. What would he have done if she hadn't died, if she had mailed a finished letter? Would he have taken her back?

He still missed and loved her, but could he forgive her? He didn't know. His emotions were conflicted. He was still angry that she had left, enraged that she had been murdered, furious at her murderer, and desperately wanting vengeance and justice.

Bobbie set the letter down and looked in the drawer. Several bank statements from Banco Nacional were there. She picked one up and looked at the account holder's name, the date, and the balance.

"Jack, here's something you won't believe. This bank statement explains more," Bobbie said. "Come over here. What do you make of this?"

"Tell me what it is," Jack said, feeling wrung out and unable to muster the strength to move.

"It looks like Becky has nearly two and a half million dollars in the bank," Bobbie exclaimed. "Jack, do you understand what this means?"

"It means she was rich, just as she said. Now I know how much," said Jack, his natural curiosity propelling him off the bed to see what Bobbie had found.

"Sure, but it means *you* are now rich," Bobbie said. "You're still married to her, so it's your money."

"I don't know. It's illegal drug money. Nobody should have it," Jack said without emotion.

"I think you should keep it. After everything you went through to help her, to save her, you deserve this," said Bobbie, trying to motivate him. "Don't forget, she put you through hell."

Jack noticed the disdain on Bobbie's face when she talked about Becky. It wasn't the first time she had given him that look. He knew she didn't think much of Becky, especially after she left him for Jamaica and Robert Mackey. He could almost read her mind.

Bobbie probably was right. He should stop feeling sorry for Becky. She did this. Was he a fool for thinking he needed to protect her when all she did was leave him twice? First for cocaine, and then again for money?

"Jack, she left Jamaica and came here because she had all this money!" Bobbie said. "I hate to say it, but that's what she cared about."

He couldn't disagree. It was what he was thinking.

"This letter makes it clear what happened," Bobbie said. "She left you in Florida for Mackey and cocaine. Then she got into trouble in Jamaica and asked you to save her. Then she changed her mind again when she learned there were two and a half million dollars in drug money here in Bogotá."

"I've had these thoughts as well, Bobbie," said Jack as he stood up. He knew she loved him, but she also loved cocaine and money.

He walked over to the desk and picked up Becky's bank statement.

"It looks like this statement was dated last month," he said. "She had all this money. No wonder she didn't come home after Jamaica."

"Jack, setting aside how awful Becky was, we need to find out more about this money, even if you don't want it," Bobbie said.

"It's getting late. Besides, it's Sunday. Let's go in the morning," Jack said. "I need time to consider all this."

Chapter 16:
Transfer Confirmed

9 a.m., Monday, Jan. 12, 1981

The following day, Jack and Bobbie walked to Banco Nacional. They met with Juan Domingas, the bank executive who handled Becky and Michelle's accounts.

"Sí, I remember the two pretty American women, Becky Kendall and Michelle Talley. I am so sorry to hear about your wife and her friend. I handled the transaction that sad day last week," Juan said. "What can I tell you?"

"What transaction?" Jack asked.

"They asked me to wire transfer most of their funds to their accounts in Sarasota," Juan said.

"How much did they transfer?" Bobbie asked.

"Nearly \$2.5 million each," Juan said.

"How much?" Jack exclaimed as he quickly stood up.

"Two and a half million," Juan repeated.

Jack stood there in disbelief. "I don't understand. Did they close their accounts?"

"They each kept $10,000. I needed special permission to do the transfers, but it was just paperwork. They were good customers," Juan said.

"I'm sure. Can you tell me to which account Becky transferred her money?" Jack asked.

"I remember it quite clearly. Becky transferred her money to the joint account she shared with you," Juan said.

Jack shook his head and sat down. He couldn't believe it. "Two and a half million dollars," he repeated.

"Jack, it's true," Bobbie said.

"I had no idea," Jack said.

"I did that for them, but I have to tell you something that happened later when she returned to withdraw $10,000," he said.

"Who came back?" asked Jack.

"Michelle Talley. Michelle closed her account more than an hour after they transferred their money. She was very nervous. Something was wrong, but she insisted everything was fine," Juan said.

Jack was stunned. He waited for Juan to explain the rest.

"I called the police and reported possible extortion. I should have stopped her from leaving. I regret I didn't do more. She insisted and was in a hurry," Juan said.

Jack shook his head in sorrow. He now realized that Becky and Michelle's deaths might have been avoided if the banker had acted differently. But he wasn't angry with Juan, only at Gordo, who he was sure was her murderer.

"Thanks for telling me what happened," Jack said.

Bobbie looked at Jack, then asked Juan, "Does Becky have

any money left in her account here?"

"Sí, I remember, it is $10,000. Mr. Kendall, you would need to file some legal papers to claim this money," Juan said.

"Can you tell me anything else Becky told you?"

"I talked mostly with Michelle," Juan said. "But they both were so happy to return to their home in Sarasota."

"And when Michelle returned, did she say anything about where she was going?" Jack asked.

"No, but she seemed upset and in a hurry," Juan said. "I'm so sorry. I should have alerted the police immediately."

Jack stood up, visibly distressed. "If you think of anything else, we are staying at her condo at least for the night, or you can contact Detective Morales."

Juan nodded. "Sí, señor."

Jack stood up and walked back to the lobby with Bobbie.

"What's wrong, Jack?" asked Bobbie as they stopped by the front desk.

"When Michelle returned to the bank for the second time, they were still alive. Gordo must have killed Becky after he realized they transferred the money to Sarasota."

"It's yours now," Bobbie replied.

"Yes, but Gordo knows I have the money," Jack said.

"He won't dare show his face in Sarasota, not with warrants out for his arrest," Bobbie assured him.

"I'm not so sure. Gordo is a crazy jackass," Jack responded.

"We'll be careful. What about the two and a half million?"

"I had no idea she did that," Jack said. "The last time I checked our joint account, it had only a few hundred dollars. I never thought to close it."

"It's only been a week. If the money is in your bank account, you have no choice but to deal with it," Bobbie said. "You'll need to talk with your lawyer friend, but two and a half million dollars can do a lot of good."

"Maybe. I'll check on this later. Let's go to the police station," Jack said. "I want to speak with the detective in charge of the murder investigation."

"We also have to identify her body," Bobbie reminded Jack.

"I know. Bobbie," Jack said, pausing, "we must consider another possibility."

"What possibility is that?" Bobbie asked.

"That if Gordo killed Becky and Michelle, he still might be in Bogotá, and he may still want that two and a half million."

"I don't see how, but we'll need to be careful," Bobbie said.

"He needs to be careful, too, because I plan on staying to help the police find him," Jack added firmly.

"Are you sure about that, Jack?" Bobbie asked. "He's dangerous."

"When I'm angry, I can be dangerous too—and I'm *angry*," Jack said, looking at Bobbie with steely eyes.

Chapter 17: Colombian Police

10 a.m., Monday, Jan. 12, 1981

Jack hurried into the heavily fortified police station, with Bobbie close behind. He wanted answers to the nagging questions that had troubled him throughout the night and the morning.

At the front desk, Jack asked if the desk sergeant spoke English.

"Sí, señor, what do you need?" the middle-aged sergeant asked.

"I'm Jack Kendall from Florida. May I speak with the detective in charge of the murder investigation of Becky Kendall and Michelle Talley?"

"That would be Detective Morales. Hold on," he said as he picked up the phone. "Matias. I have two Americans here. They want to talk with you about the Kendall/Talley murder investigation. I think it is the husband."

The sergeant hung up the phone and looked up at Jack.

"He will be right out. Have a seat over there," he motioned to a wooden bench against the wall.

"Gracias," Jack replied as he and Bobbie sat down, waiting in the quiet, tiled lobby. The place smelled of strong Colombian coffee drifting in from somewhere down the hall. A ceiling fan turned lazily overhead, doing little to chase away the humid air.

After a few minutes, the door at the end of the corridor creaked open, and the detective stepped out. He was a middle-aged man with a trim mustache and a neatly pressed suit that had seen long days.

Jack stood, shook his hand, and braced himself.

"Mr. Kendall. I am Detective Morales. I spoke with you on the phone a few days ago. I want to extend my condolences again about your wife and her friend," said Morales in a deep voice with a faint rasp.

"Thank you. Call me Jack. Do you have any suspects?"

"I will give you everything we know about our investigation, but first, I need you to identify your wife," Morales said.

"Can we do that in a minute? I have some questions I need answered right away," said Jack.

"I will answer everything, but we must follow procedure about identification," said Morales, who had a rugged appearance shaped by years in the force.

Jack closed his eyes and breathed heavily. He'd expected to have to identify Becky, but being prepared for it was another thing altogether.

"Follow me, señor." Morales led them to the morgue at the back of the station.

A mortuary assistant greeted them and directed Jack, Bobbie, and Morales into the cold storage where the bodies were held.

It was a dimly lit, sterile chamber that had a slightly antiseptic smell. Each wall had rows of stainless-steel refrigeration units that resembled oversized filing cabinets stacked on top of each other.

The assistant located Becky and slowly pulled out the metal gurney on which she was resting.

Jack hesitated to look as the assistant pulled back the white sheet. Bobbie looked at Becky first and opened her mouth in disbelief. She touched Jack's arm. He couldn't bring himself to look. He closed his eyes.

"Señor, you must identify her," Morales calmly said.

"It's okay, Jack. Just glance," Bobbie said softly.

Jack inhaled and forced himself to look upon her lifeless, pale white face. It *was* her, but her beautiful blue eyes were closed, and her magnificent, wavy red hair was neatly combed tight behind her head, neck, and shoulders. She looked cold.

He thought back to how he used to love to watch her sleep. Sometimes, she would awaken and give him a playful snarl to say, "I don't like that."

"Becky," said Jack softly, turning away after three long seconds. He didn't want to remember her this way. "It's her."

Bobbie touched Jack's arm as he slowly stepped back from the drawer with his head bowed. The assistant pushed the table away and closed the door. They left the morgue in silence.

As they walked down the hallway, the assistant reminded Jack to fill out the Consular Mortuary Certificate with the U.S. State Department and other documents for Becky's body to be flown home for burial.

Bobbie said she'd handle it. Jack wasn't paying attention. His mind was filled with grief and guilt, but mostly growing rage.

Jack followed Morales back to his office as he thought about Becky's lifeless body, so cold on that metal slab.

She didn't deserve this ending. Was he partly to blame? The realization that Becky had probably been killed because of the $2.5 million she had transferred to their joint account weighed heavily on him.

In the past few days, his emotions fluctuated from deep grief to melancholy to anger and back. Now, he felt a fierce rage simmering beneath the surface. Maybe he could have done more to find her in Colombia. But his mind was already shifting to the inevitable—how to face the monster responsible for tearing Becky away from him.

"This isn't over, Gordo. Not by a long shot," Jack muttered to himself.

"What did you say, Jack?" asked Bobbie.

Jack ignored her and asked Morales, "Will you tell me now, detective? Tell me exactly what happened to Becky. You said she was shot, all right, but how did she die?"

Bobbie was surprised by Jack's emphatic question. He wanted to know the details. She thought it was a good sign, but was it? He was starting to get aggressive. She was worried about what he had said last night about wanting to stay and help the police find her killer.

"Come with me to my office, señor," said Morales, leading the way.

Jack and Bobbie followed the detective without another word. There would be more time for mourning, but now he wanted answers.

"Have a seat, please," Morales said as they entered his office.

Jack sized up the detective. He looked professional and serious. He was in his late 40s, had a medium build, stood approximately 5 feet 10 inches tall, and weighed 180 pounds.

Jack hesitated in asking the first question. He wasn't sure he wanted to hear the exact circumstances of Becky's death, but he needed to know.

"How did she die?"

"She was shot several times in the chest," Morales said grimly. "Then Michelle Talley was shot once in the head and several other times. This is an evil man. Since she was your wife, I would be cautious if you have this money now."

"I know. Gecht tried to kill me once in Florida. Long story," Jack said, glancing at Bobbie. "I'll be careful. Now, give me the scenario of what happened."

"Based on what we've gathered in our investigation, Becky and Michelle's deaths appear to have occurred right after they transferred their money to bank accounts in America."

"I thought so, based on what the banker told us," Jack said. "But why? The money was already gone. What good did it do to kill them?"

"We believe they were killed in a fit of rage when the perpetrator realized he was too late and couldn't get access to all this money," the detective said.

"How do you know the murderer was angry?" asked Jack.

"Well, señor, it was the number of times the victims were shot," Morales said.

"How many?" Jack asked.

"He emptied his clip. Ten rounds," Morales said.

"How many times did he shoot Becky?" Jack asked.

"Jack!" shouted Bobbie, trying to stop him.

"It's okay, señorita. Mr. Kendall wants to know," Morales said. "Seven shots."

"Where was she killed?" Jack asked.

"I can't say. Sorry. It's a crime scene," Morales said.

"I understand. Thank you, detective," said Jack, turning to Bobbie. "I have to know everything. I don't want to wonder later."

"I understand. I am so sorry for your loss, señor. We are doing our best to investigate this case. It has become complicated for many reasons," Morales said.

"I want to know everything, but what about suspects? Tell me, do you know who it is?" Jack asked.

"We are looking at several suspects who came into the country days before your wife and her friend were killed," Morales said.

"It's Gordon Gecht, right?" Jack asked.

"Why, yes, he is of particular interest. He arrived in Colombia under a different name and with a fake passport that we initially overlooked. However, we have his picture, which we verified with people who recently entered the country. He is a wanted international criminal. There is an outstanding arrest warrant for him in Florida on suspicion of murder and narcotics trafficking."

"Let me see his picture," Jack said.

Morales showed him the passport picture.

"It's Gecht, the murdering bastard," said Jack, instantly recognizing him, even with the stupid black mustache disguise.

"Everybody called the son-of-a-bitch Gordo. He worked at the High Seas Restaurant with Becky," said Jack, feeling a pressure building in his chest. He needed to ask a few more questions before he exploded. "Why do you suspect he killed her?"

"We found prints at the scene of the crimes and in the rental car he used to kidnap the women. I am very sorry,"

Morales said. "We have witnesses. Everything points to Gecht; we believe he is the one."

"Of course, he's the one," Jack said, his voice filled with anger. "He killed Becky and Michelle in cold blood. We have to get him."

Detective Morales watched Jack's reaction closely, his expression grim. "If this man is the one, we're not just dealing with a common criminal. We're dealing with a dangerous predator."

"He's more than that. He's a sadist," said Jack, slamming his fist on Morales's desk, the blow bouncing objects on it into the air. "I should've known he'd come looking for them. I should've come here sooner and taken her away!"

His voice was raw, each word laced with guilt and rage. "Becky...Michelle...they're gone because of me. And he's out there walking free."

Morales stood up, his tone firm but measured. "Jack, listen to me. If Gecht is here, we'll find him."

Jack shook his head, his gaze burning with determination. "I don't care what it takes. I'll find him. And when I do, he will pay for what he's done."

Bobbie began to sniffle. She knew what Jack meant, even though Morales didn't understand the implication.

Morales placed a hand on Jack's shoulder, his voice steady. "You want justice, not vengeance. Trust me, Jack—we'll get this bastard."

Jack met the detective's eyes, his anger momentarily giving way to a flicker of hope. But deep down, he knew this wasn't just about justice. For Jack, this was personal.

"Let us know if there is anything we can do while you are here," Morales said. "We are actively searching for him. It would be best for you and Bobbie to leave as soon as possible for your safety. We do not believe he has left the country."

"Detective, originally, I had planned on leaving tomorrow morning," Jack said, standing up and looking at Morales directly. "But I've changed my mind. We're staying."

Morales walked from around his desk and stood next to Jack. "There is nothing for you to do here. You should leave. Gecht knows you have the money he sought. He could come for you. When you return to Florida, we will inform you about our progress."

"You say you know it's Gecht, so you have enough for an arrest?" Jack asked.

"Yes, we also believe he killed a cab driver in Zipaquirá, but as I said, it's complicated," Morales replied, turning his head.

"What? Why did he kill a cab driver?" Jack asked.

"We think he drove Becky and Michelle to Zipaquirá for sightseeing. Gecht killed the driver and then intended to kidnap the women there. He rented his car in that area," Morales explained, looking back at Jack. "It's our theory."

Jack listened intently. "You suspect this. Then why is it complicated to arrest him? He's killed three people, and the death toll is just beginning, believe me."

"I can't go into the details of our evidence and methods. I'm sorry; it's police business," Morales said.

"I know. Bobbie and I cover cops in Florida. We have dealt with police business and methods for years," Jack said. "I'm not asking you to divulge anything about that."

Leaning forward, Jack said, "Let me tell you. I have an idea how to draw him out."

"What do you mean?" Morales asked, a skeptical look crossing his face.

"You say Gecht killed Becky because he was upset she transferred two and a half million to my joint bank account with her in Florida, right? And he wants this money?" Jack said.

"Sí, that is my theory based on the facts," Morales said.

"I'm going to assume one of the complications is that he's hard to arrest because he's probably connected in some way with Escobar's Medellín gang, right?" Jack said.

"How do you know this?" Morales asked.

"I know from our police sources in Florida that Gecht's former boss, Robert Mackey, was supplied by Escobar. Right?" Jack said.

"You are a good reporter, Mr. Kendall," Morales said. "You have accurate information."

"Thank you. What if we made it clear that the bank transfer didn't go through as planned, that the money is still here, and that I am ready to complete the transaction on a specific date?" Jack suggested.

"No, Jack. I know what you're suggesting, and it isn't a good idea," Bobbie interjected, her tone firm.

"I agree," Morales said. "You propose using yourself as bait to draw him out?"

"Yes," Jack said. "We set a trap for Gecht to try and kidnap or capture me, just like he did with Becky, and with the evidence you have, you can arrest him."

Morales shook his head. "Señor Kendall, this is not the type of risk we can endorse. You'd be putting your life in grave danger. Gordon Gecht is not someone to toy with. He's ruthless. He could very well have the backing of Escobar, who is killing police and journalists as if they were flies."

"I'm not planning on doing it alone," Jack said. "We coordinate with your anti-narcotics unit. I'll stay in an obvious location—Becky's condo, maybe—with undercover officers nearby. We control every variable. If Gecht is still in Bogotá and desperate to get this money back, he'll take the bait. If he doesn't, we'll leave. It's the quickest way to catch him if you want to catch him."

Morales grimaced. "That's a lot to take in," he said.

Bobbie's face was pale, her voice low but insistent. "Jack, this is too risky. What if something goes wrong?"

Jack faced her, his expression determined. "Becky died because of this money. If I can bring him to justice, it's worth the risk. I can't walk away knowing he's out there and could return to Sarasota someday and hurt us."

Morales exhaled heavily and crossed his arms. "It's a dangerous plan, but the idea has some merit. Let me consult my captain to see if we can execute this safely. If we proceed, it will be under our full control, and you will follow our instructions. Understood?"

Jack nodded. "Understood."

Morales gave him a long, appraising look. "Very well. If the captain approves, we will move quickly. But make no mistake, señor, this is a high-stakes gamble."

As Morales went to his desk to make a call, Bobbie leaned close to Jack, her voice trembling. "I don't like this, Jack. Please don't let this obsession get you killed."

Jack took her hand, squeezing it softly. "I won't, Bobbie. I promise. But I have to see this through—for Becky, for Michelle, and so we can move forward."

Chapter 18:
Gordo Meets Pablo

Late Morning, Wednesday, Jan. 7, 1981

Gordo arrived by cab at the front gate of Escobar's expansive Hacienda Nápoles in Puerto Triunfo. It was a three-hour drive from Bogotá. He paid the cabbie, got out, and waited while armed guards with automatic rifles checked him for weapons.

The 7,000-acre estate was secured like a fortress, with a perimeter fence and heavily armed patrols on duty 24/7, yet it maintained a lively atmosphere.

The property featured Escobar's famed pet hippos, giraffes, camels, antelope, and other exotic animals. It also had a soccer field, a tennis court, an airstrip, and even a bullfighting arena.

As the soldiers led him to the house, Gordo saw dinosaur statues, including Brontosaurus and T. rex, scattered around artificial lakes.

After the short tour, Escobar's men led Gordo inside the white, modular Spanish colonial house, where a large, bearded man with a deep, booming voice rechecked him for weapons.

"You will soon be introduced to Pablo Escobar. This is an honor for you, and you will treat him with great respect," said the large man who appeared to be the leader of Escobar's soldiers.

Gecht wasn't sure how Robert Mackey met Pablo Escobar, but he knew they were friends because of the stories Robert would tell about the Colombian.

By the mid-1970s, Pablo Escobar co-founded the Medellín Cartel, quickly evolving from a small-time car thief into a multimillionaire by smuggling large amounts of cocaine to the U.S. and Europe. Although ruthless, killing hundreds of rivals and officials, he also gained a Robin Hood-like reputation by funding social programs and helping Colombia's poor.

As Gordo was escorted through the well-adorned house, he heard men, women, and children speaking excitedly in the next room. "Follow me," said the large man.

He walked into a large dining room where Escobar was seated at a long, glass-topped table, eating and talking with at least 20 of his family members, friends, and associates.

Gordo couldn't help but notice a giant painting of a magnificent horse—Terremoto de Manizales—that he later learned belonged to Escobar.

Under the horse painting on the far side of the room, 33-year-old Pablo Escobar sat. He looked up at Gordo and smiled.

"Welcome, Señor Gecht. I understand you have asked to meet me. I have granted you an audience because of your reputation and association with my departed friend, Robert

Mackey. He always spoke very highly of you," the drug lord said.

"I was told once by Robert that if I ever needed a job, you are the man to see," Gordo said.

"I am just a decent man who exports flowers," Escobar said dryly.

"Robert told me you also are a man who loves his wife and children and does much good by helping the poor," Gordo said.

"This is true, señor," Escobar replied. "I can replace things, but I could never replace my wife and kids."

Gordo nodded. "This is a good trait."

Escobar examined Gordo very closely. He smiled again and said, "You have good manners and special talents. Is this true, what I heard about those talents?"

"It is. Tell me what you need, and it will be done," Gordo said.

Escobar waved his hand in a sign to slow down the conversation.

"I was sorry to hear about Robert. He ran a good restaurant business in Florida and Jamaica," Escobar said.

"Yes, he did. Unfortunately, I couldn't help Robert with his problems in Jamaica," Gordo said. "I was delayed in Miami and couldn't arrive in time to make a difference."

Escobar stopped Gordo. "Please, señor, let me excuse my wife and children," he said, turning to them in Spanish. "Go play outside, my dears. I am going to talk with my new friend."

After they left, Escobar kept talking. "From what I was told, Robert was double-crossed by Lester Coke."

"I believe this to be true. I heard this from Robert's pilot, news reports and from survivors of Robert's security who escaped through the woods—the cowards," Gordo said with disgust.

Escobar shifted forward. "What did you hear?"

"Robert had a major business deal that night, one of the most important of the year. Lester Coke learned about it and was envious of Robert's success in America. He promised the Rings that if they got rid of Robert, he would give them control of distribution on the northeastern side of Jamaica, excluding Kingston, and in return, receive a 20 percent cut," Gordo said.

Escobar nodded.

"During the transfer, the Rings attacked Robert and decimated his men. But the Rings were then surprised by some patriotic Rastas who had support from the American CIA. The result was that both Robert's men and the Rings were wiped out," said Gordo, shaking his head.

"This cannot be tolerated," Escobar said.

"I'm glad to hear you feel that way," Gordo said. "Robert didn't stand a chance with two groups attacking him. It was a huge intelligence failure. Someone talked to the CIA and Coke. I don't know who."

"We will settle Lester's transgression in due time and find out who the traitor was," Escobar promised.

"What can you do? He is well-protected, and it is not your country," Gordo said.

"We have ways. Let me tell you...sometimes...there are times when I feel like God...when I order someone killed, they die the same day."

Gordo smiled. He liked Escobar's killer instincts. He could work for this man. He was loyal to his family and associates. He was all business to his enemies.

"I have several problems for you to solve, if you want them," Escobar said. "We need an American with the right touch to get things done in certain areas."

"I was hoping you'd say that," Gordo said.

"Before we get to that, I need to know if it was you who killed those two American señoritas and are on the run because of it." Escobar's voice was calm, but his eyes burned with quiet intensity.

"I did," Gordo said, shifting uneasily. "And yes, I am."

"Why did you kill them?" Escobar asked, his tone deceptively casual.

Gordo shifted nervously. "They had money that belonged to Robert and Michael," said Gordo, apprehensive about the implication of Pablo's question. "Since they are gone, I felt it should be mine."

"But you didn't get this money, did you?" said Escobar, raising a sharp eyebrow.

Gordo's gaze darted around the room, apprehensive about the weight behind the question. "No," Gordo frowned, a flash of irritation crossing his face. "It was bad timing on my part. They had already wired it to Florida."

"How did you know this?"

"They told me and showed me the bank receipt."

Escobar leaned back in his chair, studying Gordo intently. "It seems there was another reason you killed them. Please explain."

Despite Escobar's probing questions, Gordo decided to show strength in his answer. "Robert ordered me to kill them if anything ever happened to him," he said, sitting straighter in his chair.

"I see," Escobar nodded. "I must tell you I knew about these women—Becky Kendall and Michelle Talley. Robert told me they were staying with him in the Blue Mountains. He said when they finished their last job in Jamaica, they would be coming to Bogotá to rest and regroup," Escobar said.

Gordo's heart skipped a beat.

"When he arrived, we planned to discuss his future with me," Escobar continued smoothly. "His business in Jamaica and Florida was, how you say, interrupted."

"I did not know this," Gordo said, a trace of nervousness creeping into his voice.

"No matter," Escobar said with a wave of his hand. "When I heard the news about Robert's passing, I took it upon myself to watch over the señoritas. I did not know of your plans for them."

"I felt I was following Robert's wishes," Gordo said quickly, feeling defensive.

Escobar's lips curled into a faint, enigmatic smile. "Life is full of surprises, some good, some not so good. When they took that money, they discovered something not-so-good."

Gordo nodded, relaxing slightly as Escobar's tone shifted. He had taken a calculated risk by killing Becky and Michelle, and now, it seemed, Escobar saw the logic in his actions.

"Let me explain fully," Gordo said, "Becky's death is also intended to draw Becky's husband, Jack Kendall, to Bogotá."

"Who is this Jack Kendall, and why is he so important?" Escobar asked, surprised at Gordo's plan.

Gordo's jaw tightened, his gaze steady despite the tension in the room. "He is a very irritating journalist who was partially responsible for exposing Robert's business to the police," he said.

"I need to eliminate Kendall," he continued, his voice low but resolute. "It's a job Robert gave me months ago that I never got the chance to finish. Kendall's survival is a loose end—and I don't leave loose ends."

Escobar's expression shifted subtly, a flicker of interest passing across his face. He leaned forward slightly, his dark eyes glinting. "A loose end, you say?"

"Yes," Gordo said, his voice gaining confidence. "He knows too much. And as long as he's alive, he could cause problems for us."

Escobar leaned back, his fingers tapping against the armrest of his chair as he studied Gordo.

"Killing journalists is nothing to me. I also like that you followed Robert's commands even though he is no longer of this life," Escobar said, his voice turning warm. "It says a great deal about you. Because of this, I will give you work you enjoy, protect you, and allow you to earn that money back—and more—if you take care of some of my problems."

Gordo exhaled, relieved by the change of tone.

"I will," Gordo said carefully, "on one condition."

Escobar's smile vanished. "I am not a man who is given conditions," Escobar replied with a menacing laugh.

Gordo's heart pounded. "I didn't mean it like that," he said, his voice hurried. "It's not a demand, just...a request, but only if I don't have an opportunity to kill Kendall here. I want to be able to go back to Florida when it's safe for me to tie up my loose end."

Escobar nodded slowly, a faint smirk returning to his lips. "Interesting. Very well, Señor Gecht. Prove your value to me here, and when the time comes, I may grant you the freedom to tie up this...loose end."

"I would be tremendously thankful," Gordo said.

"But here is some free advice. You must be careful if you return," said Escobar. "For me, it is much better to be in a grave in Colombia than in a jail cell in the United States."

"I see what you mean, but I will not get caught here or there. I have a plan. I need a little time and money to put it in place," Gordo said.

"What is your price for handling problems I need solving?" Escobar asked.

"Name it," Gordo said.

"So you understand, I like to handle problems in two ways. 'Plata o plomo,'" said Escobar. He paused, waiting for Gordo's reaction.

"What does that mean?" Gordo asked.

Escobar smiled. "In English, it means with silver or lead."

"Plata o plomo. Yes, we did this in Florida. Bribes first, then bullets," Gordo said. "I did both, whatever Robert needed."

"Bueno," said Escobar. "We understand each other. "Now, let's drink rum, eat, and talk about the first problem I need you to solve for me."

"I like that," Gordo said as he smiled and reached out to shake Escobar's hand. "I am at your service."

Escobar reached over, then withdrew it and pointed a finger in the air.

"Always remember this: all empires are created of blood and fire, and there can only be one king."

Gordo nodded and shook the drug lord's hand. He knew he had found the right job with Escobar, and when it was finished, Kendall would be dead, either in Bogotá or back in Florida.

Chapter 19: The Informant

Late Morning, Tuesday, Jan. 13, 1981

Detective Morales greeted Jack and Bobbie in the lobby of the Bogotá station a little before 11 a.m.

"Jack, welcome. We have a break in the case. Come with me," said Morales as he motioned for them to follow.

Morales led Jack and Bobbie down a busy hall filled with officers and people sitting on benches, waiting to be booked or report crimes.

"I want to introduce you to Col. Jaime Ramírez Gómez. He signed off on your plan to capture Gecht."

"Who is Gómez?" Jack innocently inquired.

"I am glad you asked, señor. Col. Gómez is a legend in our department. He leads our anti-narcotics unit and is widely known for standing up to Cali and Medellín," Morales said. "He wants to embarrass Escobar."

Morales stopped and knocked on the door.

"Enter," said Gómez.

"Colonel, I'd like to introduce you to the journalists Jack Kendall and Bobbie Jackson. They came from Florida to identify Jack's wife, Becky Kendall, one of the American women killed, we believe, by Gordon Gecht," Morales said.

"Sí, I know the case. I am happy to meet you, Mr. Kendall and Ms. Jackson. I have heard about your articles on cocaine trafficking in Florida," Gómez said. "We need good journalists in America to expose the fallacy that cocaine is a harmless recreational drug."

"Thank you for your vote of confidence, Col. Gómez," said Jack. "We know coke is not harmless. We have crime, murders, and overdoses in our community because of it, just as you do here."

"Sí, the death of your wife is tragic. I want to help you find justice and at the same time strike a blow against Medellín and Escobar expanding his cartel," Gómez said.

"I take it you approve of my idea to draw out Gecht?" Jack asked.

"Wholeheartedly, with your complete agreement to let us do it our way," Gómez said.

"What is your plan?" Jack asked.

"I'm going to bring in Captain Horacio Carrillo to brief us on what we have learned from our informants," said Gómez, pressing a button on his desk intercom. "Captain, please come in."

The head of Bogotá's detectives, Captain Carrillo, entered the room and stood at attention until Gómez addressed him.

"At ease, Captain," Gómez said. "I should explain that Captain Carrillo was a lifelong soldier with chain-of-command habits I cannot break. Please give us your report, Horacio, in English, and feel free to contribute to the discussion."

"Yes, sir. One of our confidential informants received a tip from a source in the Medellín cartel. The CI confirmed that the Cali cartel orchestrated the attack on the Zipaquirá bus last week that killed the four American coal company workers," Carrillo said.

"While we believe the Medellín performed the hit and is trying to blame Cali, the informant identified an American in a white suit. We believe this man is Gordon Gecht, who is now working with Escobar," Carrillo said.

"What is the relevance of this information?" Gómez asked.

"In exchange for this tip, the CI's source asked if the American Jack Kendall was in Bogotá," Carrillo said.

Jack shifted his weight forward and interrupted. "Excuse me, captain. Why would the source ask this question? Wouldn't answering that violate police policy?"

"Jack, let me explain," Morales said. "May I have permission to divulge off-the-record information, Colonel?"

"You may; police corruption is not a secret," Gómez said. "We are doing our best to root it out."

"Detective Morales, you have the same look I've seen on many good cops," Jack said. "What aren't you telling me?"

"The CI believes he exchanged information with a corrupt police officer," Morales said. "He isn't corrupt, but we are using this misbelief as a backchannel to set the bait for Gecht."

"I see, so what did you tell this informant?" Jack asked.

"Thank you, Horatio," said Gómez. "I'll take it from here. We told the informant that you arrived in Bogotá three days ago, identified Becky's body, and learned the U.S. Comptroller of the Currency and international banking officials held up the $2.5 million transfer."

"Was the transaction actually delayed?" Jack asked, puzzled.

"No, the transfer was completed. The $2.5 million, I was told, is in your bank account in Sarasota," Gómez said.

"But Gecht doesn't know that," chimed in Bobbie.

"That is correct, Ms. Jackson," Morales said.

"We also told the informant that you will complete the transfer tomorrow morning after you provide the OCC with the necessary documents, which you are gathering today," Gómez said.

"Did Gecht take the bait?" Jack asked.

"We believe he did. We did not give the informant any more information or request anything more in return to avoid making Gecht suspicious," Carrillo said.

Jack nodded. "And you believe he will come for me at Becky's condo before I make the transfer," he said.

"Sí, I will be inside the condo with two of my best men," Morales said.

"We will have officers and sharpshooters from the Bogotá PD and the National Police inside and surrounding your building," Gómez said.

"What about Bobbie? I don't want her in the condo," Jack said.

"We will arrange for Bobbie to stay the night in one of the empty apartments on a different floor," Morales said. "She will be safe with two other officers. I hope this meets with your satisfaction?"

"It's perfect with me. What about you, Bobbie?" Jack asked.

"If you insist. I am fine being with Jack," Bobbie replied.

Jack shook his head. "You see what kind of a hands-on reporter she is? She doesn't want to miss out on a first-person story," he said with a smile.

The three Colombian police officers nodded and smiled

as Bobbie stared ahead, poker-faced.

"We will go over the remainder of the details in the morning, Jack," Morales said. "Do you have any questions?"

"Just one. Can you give me a weapon? I might need one for protection. He is coming for me and I'd like to be ready," said Jack, his face solemn.

Chapter 20:
The Setup

Morning, Tuesday, Jan. 13, 1981

When Gecht learned through Medellín's police informant that Jack Kendall had arrived in Bogotá, his pulse quickened with excitement and anger.

The chance to eliminate Kendall felt like destiny finally aligning. Without wasting time, he sought an audience with Pablo Escobar, presenting his case with barely contained urgency.

"El Patrón," Gecht began, his voice steady, "I have learned that Jack Kendall is here in Bogotá. He's staying at Becky Kendall's condo."

Escobar leaned back in his chair, his expression unreadable. "This man—Kendall—you've told me about him before. Is he this important to you?"

Gecht clenched his fists at his sides. "Kendall is a danger to us all. He's a journalist who digs where he shouldn't and uncovers things better left buried. Silencing him wouldn't just protect me—it would protect your operations in America. Removing him in Colombia sends a message about your greatness. May I have this honor?"

Escobar tilted his head, considering Gecht's request. "If this is something you want very badly," Escobar said calmly, "then so be it. Talk with Carlos. Take the men you need, but do it quickly. I don't like loose ends lingering in my country."

"Thank you, El Patrón," Gecht said, his voice mixed with gratitude and determination.

Later, Gecht met with Carlos Lehder Rivas, leader of Escobar's security force, in a dimly lit back room filled with maps and surveillance equipment. Carlos listened without interruption as Gecht laid out his request.

"You have permission to surveil him," Carlos said, lighting a cigarette and leaning back. "No mistakes, Gecht. If you act, it must be swift and clean. El Patrón does not tolerate complications."

Gecht nodded sharply. "I'll do it right. I'll start watching him at Becky's condo and plan the attack there. Kendall won't leave Colombia alive."

Carlos exhaled a plume of smoke, his gaze sharp. "For your sake, I hope so. Failure isn't an option when El Patrón gives you his blessing."

As Gecht turned to leave the room, Carlos stopped him. "Wait, I want you to take Jorge Cabrera. Since you are new with us, he will help you evaluate the building and identify potential risks before you enter."

"Cabrera? Isn't he in charge of our intelligence unit? Are you sure he is necessary for a journalist?" Gordo asked.

"I want him with you to make the final decision. You can have the honor of terminating Kendall, but Jorge will give you the green light to do it," Carlos said. "It's for your protection. You don't want to fail El Patrón the first time out."

Gordo sighed. The weight of Escobar's command pressed on him, but it also fueled his resolve. Jack Kendall's days were numbered, and Gecht was determined to deliver the final blow.

Chapter 21:
The Trap

Early Morning, Wednesday, Jan. 14, 1981

Gecht spent the night watching Becky's condo from an apartment across the street. Earlier, his men had surprised a family and held them at gunpoint, threatening them with death if they didn't cooperate. The apartment gave Gecht the perfect vantage point.

The cartel's six-member team, including Carlos and Jorge, gathered in tense silence, wrapped in the early morning darkness. Two weeks earlier, when he was surveilling Becky, Gecht had studied the building intensely, noting every window, alley, and escape route.

"Who's ready?" Gecht said impatiently.

"We haven't heard from our police informant," said Jorge, shaking his head. "I don't like moving without intel."

"Kendall's alone with his girlfriend," Gecht said, his tone sharp. "It's simple. We go in, kill him and anyone with him, and disappear."

Jorge gave him a skeptical look. "You sure?" he asked, his voice low.

Gecht scowled, his patience thinning. "I've been watching all night. No movement. Kendall's a sitting duck."

Jorge crossed his arms, unconvinced. "Just because we haven't seen anyone doesn't mean it isn't a trap. We don't want to be the ducks getting plucked."

Carlos chimed in, his voice gruff but resolute. "Either way, we won't move until the diversion begins," he said. "They should be here soon."

Gecht's lips curled into a thin smile. "Fine. But once we're in, there's no hesitation. We don't leave anyone alive."

* * *

As the sun rose, a sense of urgency filled the air around the condo where Jack waited along with Morales and two undercover police officers.

Down the hall, inside an empty apartment, more than ten other officers waited, each assigned to a specific role in the operation. A half dozen sharpshooters were stationed in buildings surrounding the condo.

Detective Morales led the team, ensuring that surveillance equipment was installed throughout the building, including hidden cameras and listening devices that monitored every entrance and exit. Each officer was equipped with a communication device to maintain constant contact.

Jack paced in his condo. He hadn't slept much. Bobbie was safely tucked away in an upstairs apartment with two officers protecting her.

"Matias," Jack said, "you've got us well protected, but what if Gecht doesn't show up?"

Morales, talking with Carillo, adjusted his earpiece. After getting an update on the scene outside, he smiled and walked to Jack.

"Gecht expects you to go to the bank to make the wire transfer when it opens at nine this morning, and we have just received word that three vehicles owned by Escobar have entered the city," Morales said.

"So, it's beginning?" Jack asked, eager for the trap to unfold.

Morales nodded. "I'm going to tell everyone to be ready."

"Matias, I am worried about Miguel. Are you sure he will be all right downstairs at his front desk?" Jack asked.

"Miguel insisted he not be replaced by an officer. I'm not sure I told you about him. He and I served in the military together. He is a good man and helps the police often," Morales said.

"Ah, that explains a lot. I'm still worried. I don't want anyone else getting hurt," Jack said.

"He is wearing a bulletproof vest, but we don't believe Gecht will enter the building, at least not through the front door," Morales assured him.

Jack nodded. All he could think about was stopping Gecht, whether through arrest or death. He knew he would inevitably cause trouble for many people if he managed to escape.

Outside, excitement spread among the police detail as news about Escobar's cars circulated. The officers and sharpshooters had been waiting all night, not knowing when Gecht might strike. They were itching for action.

Five minutes later, one of Escobar's cars drove slowly past the condo building. An officer stationed on a rooftop signaled Morales.

"Stay sharp," Morales whispered into his radio. "They're coming."

The vehicle passed by and parked around the corner. Another car came from the other direction and was doing the same.

On a rooftop across the street, a sharpshooter shifted for a better view as one car turned the corner. As he moved, a pack of cigarettes slipped from his shirt pocket, tumbling three stories to the pavement below.

A lookout from Gecht's crew spotted the falling pack. His gaze darted upward, and there it was: the faint silhouette of the sharpshooter.

"Jorge, we've got trouble," the lookout said in Spanish over the radio. "Los tombos on the roof."

Gecht's voice crackled back, cold and commanding. "Carlos, Louis, go confirm. Handle it quietly."

Carlos and Louis exited the apartment and carefully ascended the stairs. They attached suppressors to their weapons.

As they reached the rooftop access, Carlos signaled for Louis to cover him. Bursting through the door, they spotted the sharpshooter, who turned too late. A single muffled shot silenced him, and his body slumped to the ground.

Carlos heard a faint sound coming from the officer's earpiece. He took it out and listened carefully. Detective Morales was talking with other officers.

"It's a trap. Los tombos, everywhere," Carlos exclaimed.

In the apartment below, Gecht slammed his fist on the table, fury boiling over. "Damn, Kendall. He's working with the cops."

Jorge, always calm under pressure, placed a hand on Gecht's

shoulder. "We need to leave. You'll have another chance."

Reluctantly, Gecht nodded. "Pull the team. Now."

*   *   *

At Becky's condo, Morales received word of the rooftop incident and cursed under his breath.

"Maldición! They're onto us," he muttered, picking up his radio. "They're running. Seal off the streets."

"What happened?" Jack asked.

"Gecht killed one of our sharpshooters. He must have taken the officer's radio and learned we were waiting for him. We'll get them next time."

Jack muttered a curse under his breath and clenched his fists as he gazed out the window at the busy streets of Bogotá. "I don't know. There may not be a next time."

Chapter 22:
The Warehouse Revisited

Afternoon, Wednesday, Jan. 14, 1981

Jack and Bobbie ate lunch in the condo, discussing what to do now that Gecht was at large.

"Morales said Gecht escaped without a trace. He found the three diversion cars nearby and thinks they used backup cars to leave the city," Jack said.

"What are we going to do?" Bobbie asked.

"Carillo and Gómez are planning their next move. I doubt they include us," said Jack dejectedly. "I thought we were going to end it this morning."

Just then, there was a knock on the door.

Jack peered through the keyhole. "It's Miguel."

Miguel stood there with a long face. "I imagine, señor, you are very disappointed," he said as he walked in.

"I am. I am not sure about Bobbie," Jack said, glancing at her.

"No, I am disappointed, too," said Bobbie, shaking her head. "I thought Detective Morales had a good plan."

"Will you be leaving now?" Miguel asked.

"We aren't sure. I'm waiting to hear from Morales about what they plan on doing," Jack said.

Miguel hesitated, his expression heavy. "Señor Kendall, there is something you should know. Becky...was killed in a warehouse near the outskirts of the city. I can take you there if you want."

Bobbie was surprised by Miguel's offer. "Why would you tell Jack this?"

"I'm sorry, señorita. I thought he would like to know," Miguel said. "I was very fond of Becky and Michelle and want Gecht taken off the streets. The cartel violence is bad for our city, and I've been doing what I can to stop it."

"Would you take us there?" Jack eagerly asked.

Bobbie, who had been pacing anxiously, stopped in her tracks. "Jack, think about this. What are you going to accomplish by going there?"

Jack stared at Bobbie. "I need to see it for myself. I need to understand what happened to her."

Bobbie exchanged a worried glance with Miguel. "Then I'm coming with you."

Miguel nodded. "We can leave in ten minutes."

"One thing—do you have a gun I could use?" Jack asked.

"I have several," said Miguel.

* * *

After lunch, Detective Morales, Captain Carillo, and Col. Gómez huddled around a cluttered table at the precinct, strategizing their next move. A map of Bogotá was spread before them, and red pins marked known cartel hotspots.

"I don't believe Gecht left the city," Morales said, his voice taut with urgency. "He could try again. He hates Kendall and knows he threatens him and Escobar's operation."

Gómez nodded. "We need to keep an eye on this American. He won't sit still. He's stubborn and determined."

"I agree," Morales said. "He has told me several times since Monday that he wants to find Gecht and eliminate him in Colombia. He worries Gecht will come for him in Florida."

"We need to check on the unit watching Becky's condo. If we don't keep tabs on him, he'll start looking for Gecht alone," said Gómez.

Carillo sighed, rubbing his temples. "That's what I'm afraid of. He may be a good journalist, but he's a terrible soldier."

*　*　*

As Jack, Bobbie, and Miguel left the condo, Gecht's informant across the street picked up his phone, his eyes narrowing as he watched them climb into Miguel's car.

"They're heading east on Calle 85," the informant reported. "Kendall and two other people are in a white Renault."

Gecht grinned maliciously. "I'll take care of this."

He ordered three of Escobar's men to follow him, and they followed Miguel's car as it wove through the busy streets of Bogotá, heading to a familiar location.

*　*　*

Miguel arrived at the abandoned warehouse. He parked the car a block away to give them a view of the surroundings. Jack stepped out first, his heart pounding as he neared the rusted front door.

"Jack, are you sure about this?" Bobbie asked, her voice wavering slightly.

Jack didn't answer. He pushed the doors open, the creak echoing through the cavernous space. The warehouse was dimly lit, its shadows deep and unwelcoming.

They walked inside. "Follow me. I know the room where it happened," said Miguel respectfully.

Jack followed cautiously, pondering how Becky felt during her last steps and wondering if she knew her fate. They walked to the back of the warehouse.

"Right here," Miguel said solemnly, pointing to the room. The door was marked with yellow police tape, indicating that it was a crime scene.

Jack took a step inside. Bloodstains still marred the floor where Becky and Michelle had died.

"Dear God," Bobbie whispered, covering her mouth.

*Jack knelt, brushing his fingers across the
dark, dried blood. "This is where she fought
for her life," he said hoarsely. "I can feel it."*

* * *

Outside, Gecht saw where Miguel had parked. He drove around the back of the warehouse, knowing another spot to enter. He parked his car and motioned for his three men to follow.

"This ends now," Gecht snarled as he pulled his gun from

its shoulder holster. "Kendall dies here."

The hitmen entered the warehouse with calculated precision, and their movements were as efficient as leopards stalking their prey. Gecht paused, listening for signs of life, and smirked when faint voices carried from the room ahead.

"Just as I thought," he muttered. "The same place Becky drew her last breath. Poetic, isn't it?" He turned to his men. "Carlos, watch the back door. If you see coppers, take them out. Dandeny and Francisco, follow me."

Gecht and the others crept toward the room where Jack, Bobbie, and Miguel were talking.

"Well, well," an overconfident Gecht sneered as he entered the room.

Jack spun toward the familiar voice, his instincts kicking in.

"You should've stayed in Florida, Kendall. But I suppose you wanted to see firsthand where your two-timing, no-good, greedy wife died."

Jack quickly grabbed Bobbie and dove behind a crate as Gecht opened fire, bullets ricocheting off the crate and walls. Miguel hid behind a desk.

Bobbie let out a terrified scream, clutching Jack's arm.

Jack's eyes blazed with determination. "Stay down. Don't move."

Gecht advanced, his eyes burning with rage. "You think you can outplay me?"

Jack peered out from his cover, spotting Francisco. He fired, the shot tearing a hole in the thug's chest. Francisco crumpled to the ground, his weapon clattering away. It was like Jamaica, Jack thought, kill or be killed.

Gecht was momentarily surprised. He didn't expect Jack to have a weapon. But he retaliated quickly, firing a shot that tore through Jack's shoulder. Jack cried out, falling to his knees, his gun slipping from his grasp.

"Jack!" Bobbie screamed, reaching for him.

Despite the pain, Jack gritted his teeth and reached for his weapon. Summoning his strength, he fired again as Gecht rushed in for the kill. The bullet struck Gecht in the side. He staggered back, clutching his wound, fury etched into his face.

Just then, the blare of sirens echoed through the air, followed by the creaky sound of the rusty front door opening. Morales and fellow officers burst into the warehouse with weapons drawn.

"Police! Drop your weapons and surrender!" Morales shouted, looking around the empty front room.

At the back of the warehouse, Gecht cursed under his breath. Outnumbered, with one of his men dead, another outside, and the last helping him escape, he had to leave and get away. Clutching his bleeding side, he limped toward the exit.

"This isn't over, Kendall," he hissed before retreating.

Gecht reached his getaway vehicle with Carlos and Dandeny's help just as a police car rounded the corner. "Carlos, take them out," he barked.

Carlos raised his weapon and fired off a rapid volley of shots, forcing the police to accelerate down the street.

Miguel followed Gecht to the back door with his weapon in hand, cautious in case a hitman was covering their retreat.

Dandeny helped Gecht, his face contorted in pain, into the getaway car. Carlos jumped in, and the car sped off into the maze of Bogotá's streets.

Miguel saw the car leave, noted its direction, and fired several shots, hitting the back window. Gecht heard the shots and cursed again.

"Drive to the safe house, fast," Gecht growled in pain, his hand pressing hard against his bloodied side.

As the sirens faded behind him, Gecht stared out the window and muttered, "Kendall, you won this day, but I'll finish what I started. We'll meet again."

* * *

Morales rushed into the room. Jack was slumped against a crate, his face pale and etched with pain.

Blood seeped through his shirt, pooling beneath him. Bobbie knelt at his side, her trembling hands desperately pressing against his shoulder to slow the bleeding.

"Stay with me, Jack!" she cried, her voice breaking, tears streaming down her face. "You're not leaving me, do you hear?"

Jack groaned, his head bobbing slightly as he struggled to stay awake. His breathing was erratic.

Miguel returned, calling out, "We need an ambulance!"

"Jack!" Morales shouted, falling to his knees beside him. "Hang on, amigo. The ambulance is on its way." He turned to one of his officers. "Get those paramedics in here now!"

Bobbie's hands shook as she looked at Morales. "He's losing so much blood."

Morales touched her shoulder, saying calmly, "We've got him. Just keep the pressure on."

Jack's eyes fluttered open. His voice was weak but resolute. "I shot Gecht. Did you get him?"

"He won't go far," Morales replied. "We're watching the streets."

Jack closed his eyes, knowing that Gecht had escaped again.

Minutes later, paramedics arrived, applied bandages, and placed Jack onto a stretcher. Bobbie held onto his hand as they wheeled him out.

"Will he be all right?" Bobbie asked.

The paramedic nodded and said reassuringly, "He's lost some blood, but the shoulder wound isn't life-threatening—we'll get him stabilized."

"Jack, you scared me to death," she whispered, her voice trembling. She squeezed his hand tightly. "You're lucky to be alive."

Jack managed a faint smile. "I'm not done yet."

Chapter 23:
A Journalist's Weapon

Afternoon, Friday, Jan. 16, 1981

Bobbie stayed by Jack's side for two days as he recovered from shoulder surgery at San Juan de Dios Hospital. The bullet had torn through his deltoid muscle, fracturing part of his scapula and narrowly missing vital arteries.

Dr. Andrés Valdez, a skilled trauma specialist, told Jack that he should regain full mobility through physical therapy in four to six months. The surgical staples would stay for a week during healing, leaving only a scar.

As he lay back, Jack felt the weight of the sterile white walls pressing in on him. The hospital was more than three centuries old—one of the oldest in South America—but its age only deepened the sense of confinement. He had unfinished business gnawing at him. Becky had left \$2.5 million in their joint Sarasota account, and the thought of it wouldn't let him rest. Should he use that money to dig deeper into his investigation—or finally walk away from Bogotá for good?

When Jack finally shared his thoughts, Bobbie's response came with quiet urgency. Her expression was tight with worry.

"Jack, Becky wouldn't want you risking your life any further. You've done enough. She's gone—but you're still here. Let's go home."

Jack shook his head, his voice low but resolute. "It's not enough, Bobbie. She deserves more than this. All of Gecht's victims do."

"Señor Kendall, Bobbie is right. Sometimes, the bravest thing a man can do is walk away. Let us fight this fight now," Morales advised.

After reflecting on and considering the six-month rehabilitation period required to regain full strength, Jack decided to return to Sarasota as soon as Dr. Valdez deemed it medically safe.

"Bobbie, once I am able and back at the newspaper, I will investigate the social impact of the Medellín cartel on cocaine distribution in Florida."

Bobbie smiled. It was exactly what she wanted to hear. "I will be back at the *Herald-Tribune* before you!" she exclaimed happily.

"Maybe, but I already know my first article—a firsthand account of the criminals, Gecht and Escobar, and how casual cocaine use in America fuels violence and corruption in Colombia and other countries," Jack declared.

The day before he was discharged, Colonel Gómez and Detective Morales visited Jack.

"I understand you plan to expose the cartel to your readers in America," Gómez said.

"I do. I've learned a great deal from you both. I've got to warn people about what is coming," Jack said sincerely.

"You will be doing Colombia a great service by wielding the weapon of your pen," said Gómez.

Jack cautioned Morales that Escobar would grow stronger unless Gecht were captured, prosecuted, and imprisoned.

"We will do whatever is necessary to capture Gecht," Morales promised.

"I trust you are sincere about this, but please be careful," Jack said. "As you have seen, Gecht is a sadist and a very violent criminal."

"Sí. I will keep you informed about the investigation, and feel free to call me anytime as you write about cartels," Morales offered.

"Thank you both for your commitment to justice. Your bravery is admirable," Jack said respectfully.

Colonel Gómez and Detective Morales bowed and left the hospital room.

Jack stood up, turned to Bobbie, and said, "Let's finish packing and get the hell out of here. I've got some unfinished business in Sarasota."

"What do you mean?" Bobbie asked, looking at him with concern.

"What do you think?" Jack replied.

"Gordon Gecht?" she guessed.

"Who else?" Jack said. "We must be prepared."

"Do you think he might come back to Sarasota?" Bobbie

questioned. "Mackey and LeCare are dead, and the High Seas coke ring has been dismantled. What's left?"

"Only me," Jack paused, "and if he comes for me, I'll have a surprise for him."

How to Contact Jay B. Greene

Visit My Website and Sign Up for My Newsletters: www. jaybgreene.com

By subscribing, you'll get:

- Early sneak peeks at upcoming books
- Bonus chapters, deleted scenes and exclusive short stories
- Insider updates on Jack Kendall and Tim and Peggy Smith's worlds
- Special offers and giveaways
- Author insights and personal notes

Sign up now at: **www.jaybgreene.com**

Love My Books? Help Others Discover It!

If you enjoyed one of my Jack Kendall Mystery books or Tim and Peggy Smith Space Adventure books, please consider leaving a review on **Amazon, Barnes & Nobl**e, **or wherever you bought your book.** Your reviews help other readers discover the series—and they mean the world to me as an author.

Thanks again for reading, and I hope you'll join Jack Kendall or Tim and Peggy on their next thrilling adventures!

Pursue the Truth, **Jay B. Greene**

Other Jack Kendall Mysteries

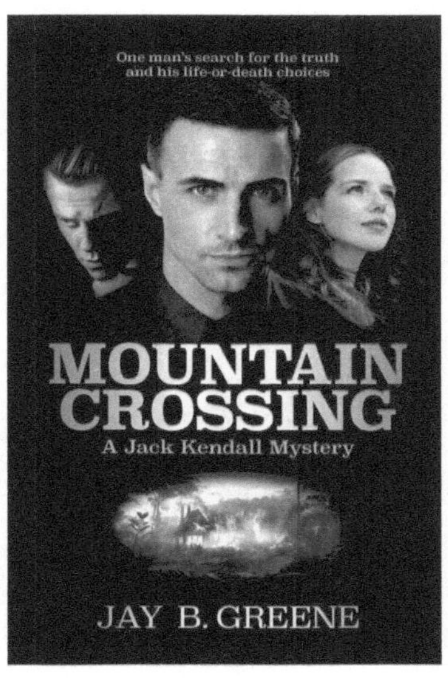

Seasoned reporter Jack Kendall is shattered after witnessing a suicide while on assignment. His life spirals further when his wife, Becky, vanishes, leaving only a cryptic letter. Driven to uncover the truth, Jack's investigation reveals Becky's ties to a dangerous global cocaine ring. With the help of Sarah, an enigmatic woman linked to his wife's disappearance, Jack ventures into Jamaica's treacherous Blue Mountains. Guided by haunting dreams of a mysterious angelic figure, Jack confronts perilous secrets about Becky's hidden life. Mountain Crossing, the gripping debut in the Jack Kendall Mystery series, is a riveting tale of love, betrayal, and survival.

Other Jack Kendall Mysteries

Investigative journalist Jack Kendall exposes the dark underbelly of Florida's phosphate industry, where corruption, environmental ruin, and murder collide. An anonymous tip leads Jack into the heart of Bone Valley's phosphate mines, where toxic spills devastate communities and powerful corporations bury the truth. Partnering with police reporter Bobbie Jackson, Jack uncovers a string of murders tied to an industry willing to kill to protect its secrets. As a Category 5 hurricane approaches, Jack faces relentless threats, including a vengeful enemy from his past. Can he survive long enough to reveal the truth? *Bone Valley*, the third Jack Kendall Mystery, is an unflinching thriller about justice, greed, and the high stakes of environmental disaster.

Jack's Next Adventure
Nokomis Hospital

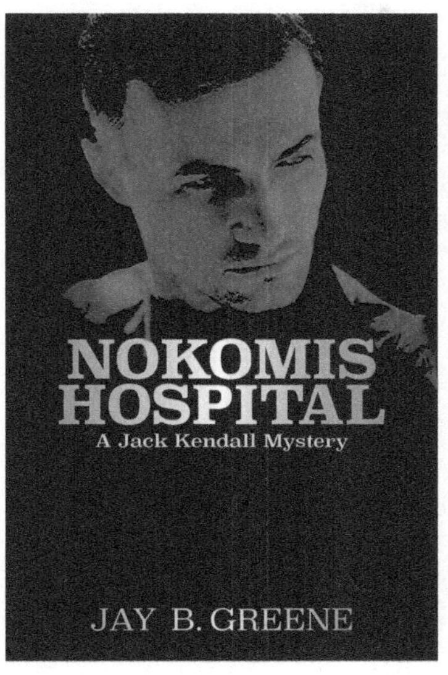

Jack Kendall suspects financial troubles and healthcare fraud when his wife, Bobbie, is admitted to Nokomis Hospital after she is treated in the ER for pre-eclampsia. While Bobbie has a successful C-section and delivers healthy twins, Jack learns from several employees during her three-day stay that charismatic CEO Mike Lard has conspired with other top executives and board members to embezzle millions of dollars that threaten the non-profit hospital's future. Join Jack as he discovers the lengths—and crimes—the executives go to cover up their illegal acts.

About the Author

Jay B. Greene was born, grew up and lives in Sarasota. He studied environmental science and journalism in college and graduated from the University of Florida. His love for stories propelled him into a 40-year career covering health care, government, crime, and the environment for several newspapers across different states.